First published in Great Britain in 2011 by Comma Press
www.commapress.co.uk
Copyright © in the name of the individual contributor
This collection copyright © Comma Press 2011

'Rag Love' by M.J. Hyland © 2010 was first published in *The Monthly*,
issue 63, Dec 2010.

'The Heart of Denis Noble' by Alison MacLeod © 2011 was first
published in *Litmus: Short Stories from Modern Science*, edited by Ra Page
(Comma, 2011).

'Wires' by Jon McGregor © 2011

'The Human Circadian Pacemaker' by K.J. Orr © 2010 was first
published in *The Bridport Prize Anthology*, Oct 2010.

'The Dead Roads' by D.W. Wilson © 2010 was first published in *PRISM
International*, issue 48:4, Summer 2010.

ISBN   1905583419
ISBN-13   978 1905583416

The publisher gratefully acknowledges the assistance of
Literature Northwest and Arts Council England across all its projects.

Set in Bembo 11/13 by David Eckersall.
Printed and bound in England by MPG Biddles Ltd.

THE BBC NATIONAL SHORT STORY AWARD

2011

Contents

Introduction

'LIFE IS TOO short for a long story,' wrote the eighteenth century traveller and woman of letters Lady Mary Wortley Montague, and we can see what she meant – she must have had her time cut out, not only with all her poetry and her insightful writing about Turkey, but also as an important early promoter of a vaccine against smallpox. She was a remarkable woman. Books were another of her passions – 'No entertainment is so cheap as reading, nor any pleasure so lasting,' she declared. So although long stories were virtually *de rigueur* in her day, I have a feeling, had she come across a shorter one, perfectly crafted, it would have been just up her street. Almost two hundred and fifty years after her death we can take equal pleasure in both a very long story and a short one. It is these briefer tales that concern us here.

What makes a good short story? My personal list of ingredients includes, obviously, a good tale distilled to its essence; then the creation of mood, not too many characters, not too much incident – though perhaps one remarkable one; and the feeling of being dropped straight into a narrative without the slow build-up that a long novel affords. It's a great test of good writing. I have been extremely lucky as the chair of the 2011 BBC National Short Story Award to have as my fellow judges three highly regarded writers – Tessa Hadley, Geoff Dyer and Joe Dunthorne – and also Di Speirs from BBC Radio Four, who has expert knowledge of the broadcast short story and of the wide sweep of contemporary writers. With the help of Booktrust and a team of readers, approximately 400 entries were whittled down to just over forty, after which we brought the forty plus down to five. It is these five stories that you read here. All the authors are already published, and some of them have won important literary prizes. Two, interestingly, come from Canadian backgrounds.

Alison MacLeod in 'The Heart of Denis Noble' has set herself an intriguing challenge, and it comes off beautifully. Denis Noble is a real person, Emeritus Professor of Cardiovascular Physiology at the University of Oxford, and a pioneer of the 'virtual' heart. He is also the main subject of this lightly fictionalised story of a scientist, also called Denis Noble, a pioneer in heart research, who is about to receive an artificial heart as a mature cardiac patient. It is touching, clever and often funny; the real Professor Noble, we are told, co-operated fully with the telling of this tale.

K.J. (Katherine) Orr's 'The Human Circadian Pacemaker' tackles another astonishing breakthrough of the twentieth century, man's ventures into space, with a wry account of an American astronaut's return home after an important mission. He can no longer communicate with his young wife, who tells the tale, but only with his space buddies, who enjoy names like Corpse, Shrink Fit and Elvis. At home, he sleeps all day. He wakes up only at night, his body clock irreversibly out of kilter. There is nothing she can do. It is a bleak tale, though there is a hint at the end of how she might find consolation in a community with a richer closeness to Mother Earth.

M.J. (Maria) Hyland's 'Rag Love' tells with the lightest of touches a story of a curious con trick perpetrated on a vast luxury liner – before it leaves port. Trudy and her partner, dressed to the nines in Sydney Harbour on a hot summer's morning, are keen to achieve their dream of making love in an on-board penthouse suite without actually clocking in as passengers. The challenge is to persuade the reluctant ship's officer showing them round to turn a blind eye. It's a will-they-won't-they page-turner, and no, I won't spoil the ending.

Jon McGregor's 'Wires' starts with a flying sugar-beet, on a motorway, heading straight towards a car windscreen. He unfolds the tale of what follows by alternating high speed and slow motion narration: it is almost filmic. We are inside the head of the young woman who has narrowly avoided a nasty accident, and possibly death. The whole story has a dream-like quality; we want her to be alright in the end, but is she? Read on...

D. W. (David) Wilson's 'The Dead Roads' is a recollection of a road trip of a very different kind, across Alberta, Canada. A young couple and their older friend Animal Brooks take to the Trans-Canada highway in a beat-up car at high speed, and then meander into the Rockies. They pick up a stranger at a gas station, and set up camp with him. From then on the atmosphere of freewheeling youthful adventure turns into something distinctly more sinister. And we are there, watching, as it happens.

Or also, in the case of these five stories, listening, for they have all made it onto BBC Radio Four. On the page, or in the ear, they make for a fine collection of tales, good evidence that the modern short story is in exceptionally good fettle.

Sue MacGregor

Rag Love

M.J. Hyland

WE STOOD IN the shade of the Orient Line ticket-booth at Circular Quay and watched the passengers leave the *Oriana*. It wasn't yet eight o'clock and already the sun was burning hot and bright.

Trudy wore a tight red dress that morning. It wasn't an evening gown, but it was long and low-cut and it showed the good and the bad of her – the roundness of her hips, the plumpness of her rear, and the growing band of her belly. I wore my best clothes, a pale blue linen suit, and a lemon shirt to go with the jacket.

I suppose we looked just the part for our plan.

Although we were skint, Trudy was certain things would soon change; that one day we'd take a luxury liner from Sydney to Southampton, the ship lit up like a private city, a thousand happy people, including us, asleep in their beds.

'It's so hot,' she said, and she took a handkerchief from her handbag and wiped her neck.

'It'll be air-conditioned on the ship,' I said.

She smiled and she was happy. 'Maybe they'll give us something to drink.'

'Yeah,' I said. 'They'll probably give us some cold lemonade.'

'Made with real lemons,' she said.

When the last passenger had left the ship, and the deckhand came with the chain to close the gangway, Trudy asked the woman at the ticket-booth if she could speak to the captain.

'We have an appointment for a private tour,' she said.

'May I have your name?'

'Mr and Mrs James Brailey.'

The woman found our booking, asked to see some identification, and told us to wait. She also told us that the captain was busy and wouldn't be able to meet us 'in person'.

'A purser will come,' she said, without looking at our faces.

Our plan was going to need a fair whack of luck. We needed to convince the purser that we were going to book a penthouse cabin on the *Oriana's* next voyage and that we were the right class of people. Once we found out where the penthouses were, we'd give our bribe to the purser so we could be left alone for a while and, when the door was locked, and we had it all to ourselves, it'd be just like we were rich passengers, and we'd make love on our luxurious bed, just the way she'd always talked about.

The night before, when we'd sat up late, Trudy told me she'd love me for all eternity and she said, 'I want to go on a big ship with you more than anything in the world.' And I told her I wanted exactly what she wanted. But the money we'd saved to pay the purser could have paid our rent and most of our bills, and I suppose I knew it was all a stupid pipe-dream. And yet, I went along for her. I wanted to go on the private tour of the liner, and pretend to be rich, because I wanted to do it all with her. I didn't tell her that I was certain she'd want the money and the ocean cruise no matter what bloke she was with. I wanted it because she wanted it, so we could have it together. But I felt sick with the certainty that she just wanted *it*, and would want it even if her husband was a different husband.

We didn't have to wait long for a purser to fetch us.

'I'm sorry for the delay,' he said.

Even though he had acne, some of it swollen and red near his mouth, his English accent made him seem handsome and better than me.

'It's been no nuisance at all,' said Trudy, in a posh voice, an accent more like the purser's.

We walked up the gangway, and Trudy held my hand as we passed the sign that said 'NOTICE

TO PASSENGERS – THE SHIP STOPS AT
SYDNEY HARBOUR FOR FOUR HOURS.
ARRANGEMENTS SHOULD BE MADE TO
RETURN TO THE SHIP BY NOON.'

The purser stopped walking and turned
round.

'Was there anything special you wanted to
see?'

Trudy told him she 'especially' wanted to see
the swimming pool and the grand ballroom.

'Then we'll start with the swimming pool,'
he said.

Trudy smiled and let go of my hand, but
gently; she passed my hand back to me so it
wasn't left to fall or drop, as though my hand was
something being safely returned. She was happy
and, for a moment, I was happy too.

★

We shared our street with the MORNFLAKE
factory and some of the men who worked on the
shop floor lived nearby. On the corner there was a
half-way house for ex-prisoners and the homeless,
with blokes that sat outside on deck-chairs, with
no shirts on, smoking roll-ups and staring at us
with their hurt faces.

We weren't as well-off as our next-door
neighbour who had just bought a flashy new
American car, but we weren't as badly off as the
woman who lived in the weatherboard on the

corner who used an old rope for walking her dog. And we weren't as strapped for cash as the skinny red-headed man who lived in a two bedroom flat above ours with his four children. He'd put his fist through the screen door a week before we went to see the *Oriana*, and the flies were getting into our flat. We were waiting for LJ Hooker to come and fit a new screen.

Our one-bedroom flat was on the ground floor and the foyer wasn't much to speak of: a side table where the mail was kept, and an umbrella stand at the base of the dirty carpeted staircase which led to the upper floors. The paint needed a fresh coat and the plants needed watering.

Most summer mornings we heard the two little boys next door splashing about in their swimming pool, a sound that made us both feel tired and sad. On a very hot day, the sight of the boys' wet footprints on the footpath made me yearn for the relief of that backyard swimming pool, and sometimes I wanted what they had so much it made me angry. At night, if our back door was open, we could hear the neighbour's little black dog drinking out of the cool water. We once went out to look over the fence and we saw the dog drinking. Just the dog, and the stars in the sky, and Trudy said, 'I'm jealous of that dog' and I said, 'Yeah, me too. But we'll get our own swimming pool one day.' I said it too often. It was a promise I couldn't keep.

*

The first passageway on the middle deck was like a street and there were signs – made to look like road signs – with arrows pointing to 'THE DECKS' and 'THE POOL' and 'THE BOATS'.

'Would you like to go up to the swimming pool via the dining room?' asked the purser.

'Yes,' I said. 'That sounds very good.'

The purser took us through the dining room, and stopped to let us look round.

'It's so very lovely in here,' said Trudy.

The circular dining tables were being set for lunch and a waiter, crouched on his haunches, used a small black brush to clean the upholstered seats. He brushed just the way a shoe-shine man does, with quick, strong strokes towards his body.

'Which is the captain's table?' asked Trudy.

'That depends,' said the purser. 'Sometimes he likes to be near the kitchen and sometimes he likes to be near the portholes so he can keep an eye on the weather.'

On the way to the upper deck, there were more signs, pointing to 'HAIRDRESSER' and 'CASINO' and 'FASHION BOUTIQUES' and every new sign made me feel hungry.

As we walked along a passageway, with doors on both sides leading to cabins, an Indian boy with a feather duster on a long pole walked ahead of us and he wiped the tops of the doors, and the door handles. Trudy smiled at me, a delighted smile; happy to be in a place where luxury afforded a boy whose one and only job was to keep the doors dust-free.

At the top of the grand staircase, the purser opened a door to the upper deck, and we were in a different world: fierce daylight and a piercing rush of heat, and the swimming pool, a perfect rectangle of sparkling blue, and on the decking, neat rows of yellow and red deckchairs and banana lounges, and two enormous red and yellow sun umbrellas.

At the far end of the pool, a young man was bouncing on the end of the diving board, but he stopped when he saw the purser and the two young women watching him, both with their backs to us, and laughed. One of them wasn't wearing her bikini top and her bare back had been burnt by the sun.

'Go on,' said the topless girl to the young man. 'I want to see you jump up and down.'

The young man looked at us and shook his head.

'Not now,' he said.

Without looking over her shoulder, the girl sensed she was being watched and reached down for the towel at her feet.

The purser coughed.

'Sometimes not all the passengers get off the ship,' he said, and turned away.

The ballroom was being prepared for a party. There was a piano on the stage and the curtains matched the upholstery on the chairs. There were three men on stepladders arranging streamers and balloons.

'Is it a special occasion?' asked Trudy, her voice gentle, and her accent like the man who reads the ABC news.

'It's a twenty-first birthday party for one of our guests.'

'It looks absolutely lovely,' said Trudy. 'And the food smells divine.'

I couldn't smell any food, but I nodded. She looked so beautiful and she'd done such a good job at sounding the part, but now she was overdoing it a bit. I wished she'd calm down.

'All the food served on the *Oriana* is of the highest quality,' said the purser, 'and the first class menu was designed by the head chef at the London Ritz.'

'How wonderful,' said Trudy.

The purser looked over my shoulder, probably at a clock.

'Was there anything else you needed to see?'

Trudy told him that we'd be paying our deposit on a penthouse suite next week, and that we'd board the ship in England, after we'd taken a train through Europe with stops in Paris and Rome. The purser nodded politely all through the far-fetched things she said.

'We'll be celebrating our first wedding anniversary on board,' I said. 'And we want to cross the seas in style.'

Trudy took hold of my hand and squeezed my fingers, nervous and excited.

'But before we make the final arrangements,' she said, 'we'd like to look inside one of the penthouses.'

She said just what we'd planned she should say, but the purser didn't respond as we'd hoped, and our dumb plan seemed at an end.

'I'm afraid that's not possible,' he said. 'I can only show you a penthouse if you've already booked your passage.'

'We thought it would be wise to see a cabin first,' I said. 'We'd like to be sure.'

'We're comparing,' said Trudy. 'We're also considering one of the new Cunard liners.'

The purser looked at Trudy and closed his mouth, as though to stop himself. He didn't believe we could afford to travel first-class and I was embarrassed by this, but even more embarrassed that I didn't realise he'd probably thought it from the moment he clapped eyes on us.

I let go of Trudy's hand.

'We have four penthouses,' he said. 'But I'm afraid I can't show you through. I'd be happy to show you some brochures though.'

'Would it be awfully inconvenient if we had a quick peek?' said Trudy.

'We have a very strict privacy policy,' said the purser.

Trudy looked down at the carpet, then back up.

'But there's nobody on board. Maybe we could just see a first-class cabin on the same deck as the penthouses? Maybe one that has nobody in it?'

And again, the purser opened then closed his mouth.

'OK,' he said. 'I think there's an unoccupied cabin on A Deck,' he said. 'But we'll need to be quick.'

He took a bunch of keys from his pocket and walked on.

The passageway on A Deck was the nicest yet; wider than the others, with wood-panelled walls, and flowers in vases on sideboards, and bowls of fruit, and platters with chocolates wrapped in silver and gold foil, and magazines, and mirrors all along the way, and the carpet was soft and thick. There were Oriental rugs too.

Two of the first-class cabin doors had been left open by the maids who were inside cleaning and changing sheets on the beds.

'Is that one of the penthouses?' asked Trudy.

'No,' said the purser, 'that's a standard first-class cabin. The penthouses are quite a bit larger and they afford very many more luxuries.'

He stopped outside cabin 18 and knocked.

'Just a precaution,' he said.

He went in and we followed.

There was a four-poster bed, a dressing table, two red leather wing chairs, a desk, and a small leather couch.

'In first-class cabins and the penthouses,' said the purser, 'there's a button just above the headboard and you can ring it any time for the steward.'

Trudy stood close to the bed and looked for the button.

'I've found it!' she said.

I wanted to take Trudy aside, hold her tight, and tell her the plan wasn't working, but that I still loved her and we should get off the ship. But I couldn't do that. So long as she didn't know he was laughing at us, maybe it didn't do any harm.

'There's 24-hour room service for first-class passengers,' said the purser.

'That sounds just the ticket,' I said.

Trudy went on looking at the room service button like an excited child and the purser and I stood behind her. I hoped he'd at least notice how lovely she was, her long blonde hair, her lovely waist, her skinny ankles.

'I'd like one of these buzzers at home,' she said. 'It'd make life a lot easier for our maid and I wouldn't have to holler all the time.'

The purser looked at the back of Trudy's

dress and pulled his chin in. He was only a purser and he thought he was my superior.

'What other facilities do you offer first-class passengers?' I said, as I ran my hand across one of the bed's corner posts, as though checking to see that the wood was solid oak, or some such.

The purser moved towards the door, making it clear he wanted us to follow.

'Well, there's dinner at the captain's table every night, of course, and a cocktail lounge, and there's a hospital, with a three-bed private ward.'

He looked at his watch.

'Is there an ensuite bathroom in all the rooms?' asked Trudy.

Her posh accent had slipped a little.

'Of course, madam,' he said. 'All the rooms on A Deck have ensuite bathrooms.'

Trudy sighed.

'It would be so very nice to see a penthouse,' she said. 'We were really hoping that we could see one today. Before we make our minds up.'

'I'd like to oblige,' he said, 'but I'm not at liberty to do that.'

'I understand,' I said. 'Your hands are tied without the permission of your superiors.'

The purser looked at me. It was, I think, the first time he'd made proper eye-contact.

'We have brochures with plenty of photographs in them. I'll get you one on the way out. And once you've paid your deposit, then we'd be more than happy to give you a guided tour.'

Trudy walked to the door and stood close to the purser, opened her handbag, and took out the cash. Even at a glance he'd have seen it was worth about a week's salary. But he stepped away.

'That won't be necessary,' he said.

He was looking at me now, suddenly curious, and something had changed.

Trudy held out the cash: three months of scrounging, some lies, and a loan from my father to cover our bills.

But he didn't take the money.

I stepped forward.

'Look,' I said, 'there must be an empty penthouse. All four of them can't be booked. And we're giving you a good lot of money here.'

I took the cash from Trudy and held it out for him to inspect.

'Take it,' I said. 'We'll only be ten minutes.'

'And we won't do anything bad,' said Trudy. 'And if we did, you could call the police. You have our names and address and everything.'

And then, just when I was sure he wouldn't, he took the money, shoved it straight into the top pocket of his jacket and said, in an unnaturally loud and angry voice, 'Please disembark immediately!'

We watched him walk to the end of the corridor, pause a moment, then turn right.

'We did it!' said Trudy. 'He took it!'

I wanted her to keep her voice down, but I said nothing and we went into the cabin. Once we'd locked the door, we stood side by side in silence and were amazed.

The penthouse foyer was like the entrance to a grand house and there were three more doors, to three more rooms; two on the left and one on the right and, straight ahead of us, beyond the opened French doors, a living room with two white leather settees, a desk, two armchairs and a round glass coffee table, and two large port-holes with views of the magnificent sky. The penthouse suite was at least twice the size of our flat.

'This is all ours now,' said Trudy. 'Isn't it wonderful?'

I told her I agreed, but I was nervous, and I wanted to promise her I'd get the money back and that we should leave.

'Which way first?' she said.

But it was too late. I went along with our mistake.

'The bedroom,' I said.

The room was immaculate and modern and so clean – the white quilt, the white pillows, the drapes, the carpet, the rugs – it was as though none of it had been used before, everything new and in perfect order. It seemed as though we were the first and only people to have ever set foot inside.

Trudy opened the door to the ensuite bathroom.

'Oh, it's true,' she called out. 'There are heated towel rails and a claw-foot bath tub.'

She came back to me holding a bar of soap shaped like the head of a rose.

'You should put that back,' I said.

She said she would, but when she came back to me, smiling, I knew she'd put it in her handbag.

'We should start,' I said. 'How will we do it?'

'Let me think,' she said.

Trudy lay on the bed and acted as though we had all the time in the world.

I wanted to get it over with, but I knew she wouldn't want it that way.

'Remember that idea we once had?' she said. 'Remember the idea that we would pretend to be a famous couple having an affair?'

'Yeah, I think so.'

She was waiting for me to get undressed, I thought, and get on the bed with her, but I wasn't sure. My heart was in my throat with panic.

'Do you remember?'

I didn't answer. I didn't remember.

I looked round behind me at nothing.

'Stop worrying,' she said. 'Don't be nervous. It's not even ten o'clock yet. And we've locked the door.'

'What do you want to do?' I asked.

She closed her eyes and lifted her dress.

'I'm alone in the room and my husband's still in the restaurant a few tables away from your wife, so that's why we've got to be quick.'

'OK.'

'You go outside and wait a few moments and then come back in, like an intruder.'

I didn't see why it couldn't just be me and Trudy this time, without the fantasy, without the other parts.

'Can't we just be us?' I said.

She kept her eyes closed and shook her head.

'But it's better this way,' she said. '*Please.*'

So I went outside to the foyer, waited a few moments then went back in. Trudy had drawn the curtains and, in the half-light, she looked incredibly beautiful.

But we rushed. And it wasn't just me. It was the both of us. Nothing was right about it. Nothing. Nothing about it was as good as it was meant to be. And not just because we rushed, and not just because we had to move to the floor half-way; there was something else. Trudy didn't talk us through it, like she usually did. She was stony quiet and she kept her eyes closed, tight, not relaxed. When we finished, she told me how good it felt, and she sounded like an actress when she said, 'It was just perfect.'

I knew it had gone wrong because it had all been made real, all the hoping and dreaming and fantasy had been made real and it was nothing, and I knew neither of us would admit it.

I stood, and she stood, and I took a towel from the bathroom to clean up, and she straightened the pillows.

We didn't speak.

On the way to the door, she looked back inside and I looked back too and, the things in the penthouse – the opened French doors, the beautiful white leather furniture, the cushions, and carpet, and coffee table and curtains – now these things looked like junk.

We went outside and walked back through the ship the way we'd come. We walked in silence along the boulevard with the grand shops and past the lovely patisserie that hadn't been open before, with its smell of cakes and baking bread and a little café table outside, and along the landing which looked down over the grand staircase, and out onto the upper deck where the red and yellow deckchairs waited in clean queues, and then down the gangway, with its glorious view of Circular Quay and, as we walked, we didn't look at each other. Not once. And over the next few days, as things fell apart – and things fell apart fast – I don't remember if we looked at each other again, and we hardly said a word.

The Heart of Denis Noble

Alison MacLeod

As DENIS NOBLE, Professor of Cardiovascular Physiology, succumbs to the opioids – a meandering river of fentanyl from the IV drip – he is informed his heart is on its way. In twenty, perhaps thirty minutes' time, the Cessna air ambulance will land in the bright, crystalline light of December, on the small landing-strip behind the Radcliffe Hospital.

A bearded jaw appears over him. From this angle, the mouth is oddly labial. Does he understand? Professor Noble nods from the other side of the ventilation mask. He would join in the team chat but the mask prevents it, and in any case, he must lie still so the nurse can shave the few hairs that remain on his chest.

No cool-box then. No heart on ice. This is what they are telling him. Instead, the latest technology. He remembers the prototype he was once shown. His new heart will arrive in its own

19

state-of-the-art reliquary. It will be lifted, beating, from a nutrient-rich bath of blood and oxygen. So he can rest easy, someone adds. It's beating well at 40,000 feet, out of range of all turbulence. 'We need your research, Professor,' another voice jokes from behind the ECG. 'We're taking no chances!'

Which isn't to say that the whole thing isn't a terrible gamble.

The nurse has traded the shaver for a pair of nail-clippers. She sets to work on the nails of his right hand, his plucking hand. Is that necessary? he wants to ask. It will take him some time to grow them back, assuming of course he still has 'time'. As she slips the pulse-oximeter over his index finger, he wonders if Joshua will show any interest at all in the classical guitar he is destined to inherit, possibly any day now. According to his mother, Josh is into electronica and urban soul.

A second nurse bends and whispers in his ear like a lover. 'Now all you have to do is relax, Denis. We've got everything covered.' Her breath is warm. Her breast is near. He can imagine the gloss of her lips. He wishes she would stay by his ear forever. 'We'll have you feeling like yourself again before you know it.'

He feels he might be sick.

Then his choice of pre-op music – the second movement of Schubert's Piano Trio in E-Flat Major – seems to flow, sweet and grave, from her mouth into his ear, and once more he can see past the red and golden treetops of Gordon Square to his attic room of half a century ago. A recording of the Schubert is rising through the floorboards, and the girl beside him in his narrow student bed is warm; her lips brush the lobe of his ear; her voice alone, the whispered current of it, is enough to arouse him. But when her fingers find him beneath the sheet, they surprise him with a catheter, and he has to shut his eyes against the tears, against the absurdity of age.

The heart of Denis Noble beat for the first time on the fifth of March, 1936 in the body of Ethel Noble as she stitched a breast pocket to a drape-cut suit in an upstairs room at Wilson & Jeffries, the tailoring house where she first met her husband George, a trainee cutter, across a flashing length of gold silk lining.

As she pierced the tweed with her basting needle, she remembered George's tender, awkward kiss to her collarbone that morning, and, as if in reply, Denis's heart, a mere tube at this point, beat its first of more than two billion utterances – da dum. Unknown to Ethel, she was twenty-one days pregnant. Her thread dangled briefly in mid-air.

Soon, the tube that was Denis Noble's heart, a delicate scrap of mesoderm, would push towards life. In the dark of Ethel, it would twist and grope, looping blindly back towards itself in the primitive knowledge that circulation, the vital whoosh of life, deplores a straight line. With a tube, true, we can see from end to end, we can blow clear through or whistle a tune – a tube is nothing if not straightforward – but a loop, a *loop*, is a circuit of energy understood only by itself.

In this unfolding, intra-uterine drama, Denis Noble – a dangling button on the thread of life – would begin to take shape, to hold fast. He would inherit George's high forehead and Ethel's bright almond-shaped, almost Oriental, eyes. His hands would be small but unusually dexterous. A birthmark would stamp itself on his left hip. But inasmuch as he was flesh, blood and bone, he was also, deep within Ethel, a living stream of sound and sensation, a delicate flux of stimuli, the influence of which eluded all known measure, then as now.

He was the cloth smoothed beneath Ethel's cool palm, and the pumping of her foot on the pedal of the Singer machine. He was the hiss of her iron over the sleeve press and the clink of brass pattern-weights in her apron pocket. He was the soft spring light through the open window, the warmth of it bathing her face, and the serotonin surging in her synapses at the sight of a magnolia tree in flower. He was the manifold sound-waves of passers-by: of motor cars hooting, of old men hawking and spitting, and delivery boys teetering down Savile Row under bolts of cloth bigger than they were. Indeed it is impossible to say where Denis stopped and the world began.

★

Only on a clear, cloudless night in November 1940 did the world seem to unstitch itself from the small boy he was and separate into something strange, something other. Denis opened his eyes to the darkness. His mother was scooping him from his bed and running down the stairs so fast, his head bumped up and down against her shoulder.

Downstairs, his father wasn't in his armchair with the newspaper on his lap, but on the sitting room floor cutting cloth by the light of a torch. Why was Father camping indoors? 'Let's sing a song,' his mother whispered, but she forgot to tell him which song to sing.

The kitchen was a dark place and no, it wasn't time for eggs and soldiers, not yet, she shooshed, and even as she spoke, she was depositing him beneath the table next to the fat yellow bundle that was his sister, and stretching out beside him, even though her feet in their court shoes stuck out the end. 'There, there,' she said as she pulled them both to her. Then they turned their ears towards a sky they couldn't see and listened to the planes that droned like wasps in the jar of the south London night.

When the bang came, the floor shuddered beneath them and plaster fell in lumps from the ceiling. His father rushed in from the sitting room, pins still gripped between his lips. Before his mother had finished thanking God, Denis felt his legs propel him, without permission, not even his own, to the window to look. Beneath a corner of the black-out curtain, at the bottom of the garden, flames were leaping. 'Fire!' he shouted, but his father shouted louder, nearly swallowing his pins – 'GET AWAY from the window!' – and plucked him into the air.

They owed their lives, his mother would later tell Mrs West next door, to a cabinet minister's suit. Their Anderson shelter, where they would have been huddled were it not for the demands of bespoke design, had taken a direct hit.

That night, George and a dicky stirrup-pump waged a losing battle against the flames until neighbours joined in with rugs, hoses and buckets of sand. Denis stood behind his mother's hip at the open door. His baby sister howled from her Moses basket. Smoke gusted as he watched his new red wagon melt in the heat. Ethel smiled down at him, squeezing his hand, and it seemed very odd because his mother shook as much as she smiled and she smiled as much as she shook. It should have been very difficult, like rubbing your tummy and patting your head at the same time, and as Denis beheld his mother – her eyes wet with tears, her hair unpinned, her arms goose-pimpled – he felt something radiate through his chest. The feeling was delicious. It warmed him through. He felt light on his toes. If his mother hadn't been wearing her heavy navy blue court shoes, the two of them, he thought, might have floated off the doorstep and into the night.

At the same time, the feeling was an ache, a hole, a sore inside him. It made him feel heavy. His heart was like something he'd swallowed that had gone down the wrong way. It made it hard to breathe. Denis Noble, age four, didn't understand. As the tremor in his mother's arm travelled into his hand, up his arm, through his armpit and into his chest, he felt for the first time the mysterious life of the heart.

He had of course been briefed in the weeks prior to surgery. His consultant, Mr Bonham, had sat at his desk – chins doubling with the gravity of the situation – reviewing Denis's notes. The tests had been inconclusive but the 'rather urgent' need for transplantation remained clear.

Naturally he would, Mr Bonham said, be familiar with the procedure. An incision in the ribcage. The removal of the pericardium – 'a slippery business, but routine'. Denis's heart would be emptied, and the aorta clamped prior to excision. 'Textbook.' The chest cavity would be cleared, though the biatrial cuff would be left in place. Then the new heart would be 'unveiled – voilà!', and the aorta engrafted, followed by the pulmonary artery.

Most grafts, Mr Bonham assured him, recovered normal ventricular function without intervention. There were risks, of course: bleeding, RV failure, bradyarrhythmias, conduction abnormalities, sudden death...

Mr Bonham surveyed his patient through his half-moon specs. 'Atheist, I presume?'

'I'm afraid not.' Denis regarded his surgeon with polite patience. Mr Bonham was widely reputed to be one of the last eccentrics still standing in the NHS.

'A believer then. Splendid. More expedient at times like this. And fear not. The Royal Society won't hear it from me!'

'Which is perhaps just as well,' said Denis, 'as I'm afraid I make as poor a "believer" as I do an atheist.'

Mr Bonham removed his glasses. 'Might be time to sort the muddle out.' He huffed on his specs, gave them a wipe with a crumpled handkerchief, and returned them to the end of his nose. 'I have a private hunch, you see, that agnostics don't fare quite as well in major surgery. No data for *The Lancet* as yet but' – he ventured a wink – 'even so. See if you can't muster a little... certainty.'

A smile crept across Denis's face. 'The Buddhists advise against too much metaphysical certainty.'

'You're a Buddhist?' A Buddhist at Oxford? At Balliol?

Denis's smile strained. 'I try to keep my options open.'

'I see.' Mr Bonham didn't. There was an embarrassment of categories. A blush spread up his neck, and as Denis watched his surgeon shuffle his notes, he felt his chances waver.

The *allegro* now. The third movement of the Piano Trio – *faster, faster* – but the Schubert is receding, and as Denis surfaces from sleep, he realises he's being whisked down the wide, blanched corridors of the Heart Unit. His trolley is a precision vehicle. It glides. It shunts around corners. There's no time to waste – the heart must be fresh – and he wonders if he has missed his stop. Kentish Town. Archway. Highgate. East Finchley. The names of the stations flicker past like clues in a dream to a year he cannot quite summon. Tunnel after tunnel. He mustn't nod off again, mustn't miss the stop, but the carriage is swaying and rocking, it's only quarter past five in the morning, and it's hard to resist the ramshackle lullaby of the Northern Line.

West Finchley. Woodside Park.

1960.

That's the one.

It's 1960, but no one, it seems, has told the good people of Totteridge. Each time he steps onto the platform at the quaint, well swept station, he feels as if he has been catapulted back in time.

The slaughterhouse is a fifteen-minute walk along a B-road, and Denis is typically the first customer of the day. He feels under-dressed next to the workers in their whites, their hard hats, their metal aprons and steel-toed Wellies. They stare, collectively, at his loafers.

Slaughter-men aren't talkers by nature, but nevertheless, over the months, Denis has come to know each by name. Front of house, there's Alf the Shackler, Frank the Knocker, Jimmy the Sticker, Marty the Plucker, and Mike the Splitter. Frank tells him how, years ago, a sledge-hammer saw him through the day's routine, but now it's a pneumatic gun and a bolt straight to the brain; a few hundred shots a day, which means he has to wear goggles, 'cos of all the grey matter flying'. He's worried he's developing 'trigger-finger', and he removes his plastic glove so Denis can see for himself 'the finger what won't uncurl'.

Alf is brawny but soft-spoken with kind, almost womanly eyes. Every morning on the quiet, he tosses Denis a pair of Wellies to spare his shoes. No one mentions the stink of the place, a sharp kick to the lungs of old blood, manure and offal. The breeze-block walls exhale it and the floor reeks of it, even though the place is mopped down like a temple every night.

Jimmy is too handsome for a slaughterhouse, all dirty blond curls and American teeth, but he doesn't know it because he's a farmboy who's never been further than East Finchley. Marty, on the other hand, was at Dunkirk. He has a neck like a battering ram and a lump of shrapnel in his head. Every day, at the close of business, he brings his knife home with him on the passenger seat of his Morris Mini-Minor. He explains to Denis that he spends a solid hour each night sharpening and sanding the blade to make sure it's smooth with no pits. 'An' 'e wonders,' bellows Mike, 'why 'e can't get a bird!'

Denis pays £4 for two hearts a day, a sum that left him stammering with polite confusion on his first visit. At Wilson and Jeffries, his father earns £20 per week.

Admittedly, they bend the rules for him. Frank 'knocks' the first sheep as usual. Alf shackles and hoists. But Jimmy, who grasps his sticking knife – Jimmy, the youngest, who's always keen, literally, to 'get stuck in' – doesn't get to slit the throat and drain the animal. When Denis visits, there's a different protocol. Jimmy steps aside, and Marty cuts straight into the chest and scoops out 'the pluck'. The blood gushes. The heart and lungs steam in Marty's hands. The others tssk-tssk like old women at the sight of the spoiled hide, but Marty is butchery in motion. He casts the lungs down a chute, passes the warm heart to Denis, rolls the stabbed sheep down the line to Mike the Splitter, shouts 'Chop, chop, ha ha' at Mike, and waits like a veteran for Alf to roll the second sheep his way.

Often Denis doesn't wait to get back to the lab. He pulls a large pair of scissors from his hold-all, grips the heart at arm's length, cuts open the meaty ventricles, checks to ensure the Purkinje fibres are still intact, then pours a steady stream of Tyrode solution over and into the heart. When the blood is washed clear, he plops the heart into his Thermos and waits for the next heart as the gutter in the floor fills with blood. The Tyrode solution, which mimics the sugar and salts of blood, is a simple but strange elixir. Denis still can't help but take a schoolboy sort of pleasure in its magic. There in his Thermos, at the core of today's open heart, the Purkinje fibres have started to beat again in their Tyrode bath. Very occasionally, a whole ventricle comes to life as he washes it down. On those occasions, he lets Jimmy hold the disembodied heart as if it is a wounded bird fluttering between his palms.

Then the Northern Line flickers past in reverse until Euston Station re-appears, where Denis hops out and jogs – Thermos and scissors clanging in the hold-all – down Gower Street, past the main quad, through the Anatomy entrance, up the grand, century-old staircase to the second floor, and into the empty lab before the clock on the wall strikes seven.

In the hush of the Radcliffe's principal operating theatre, beside the anaesthetised, intubated body of Denis Noble, Mr Bonham assesses the donor heart for a final time.

The epicardial surface is smooth and glistening. The quantity of fat is negligible. The aorta above the valve reveals a smooth intima with no atherosclerosis. The heart is still young, after all; sadly, just seventeen years old, though – in keeping with protocol – he has revealed nothing of the donor identity to the patient, and Professor Noble knows better than to ask. The lumen of the coronary artery is large, without any visible narrowing. The muscular arterial wall is of sound proportion.

Pre-operative monitoring has confirmed strong wall motion, excellent valve function, good conduction and regular heart rhythm.

It's a ticklish business at the best of times, he reminds his team, but yes, he is ready to proceed.

In the lab of the Anatomy Building, Denis pins out the heart like a valentine in a Petri dish. The buried trove, the day's booty, is nestled at the core; next to the red flesh of the ventricle, the Purkinje network is a skein of delicate yellow fibres. They gleam like the bundles of pearl cotton his mother used to keep in her embroidery basket.

Locating them is one thing. Getting them is another. It is tricky work to lift them free; trickier still to cut away sections without destroying them. He needs a good eye, a small pair of surgical scissors, and the steady cutting hand he inherited, he likes to think, from his father. If impatience gets the better of him, if he sneezes, if his scissors slip, it will be a waste of a fresh and costly heart. Beyond the lab door, an undergrad class thunders down the staircase. Outside, through the thin Victorian glass panes, Roy Orbison croons 'Only the Lonely' on a transistor radio.

Denis drops his scissors and reaches for a pair of forceps. He works like a watchmaker, lifting another snipped segment free. A second Petri dish awaits. A fresh bath of Tyrode solution, an oxygenated variety this time, will boost their recovery. If all goes well, he can usually harvest a dozen segments from each heart. But the ends will need to close before the real work can begin. Sometimes they need an hour, sometimes longer.

Coffee. He needs a coffee. He boils water on the Bunsen burner someone pinched from the chemistry lab. The instant coffee is on the shelf with the belljars. He pours, using his sleeve as a mitt, and, in the absence of a spoon, uses the pencil that's always tucked behind his ear.

At the vast chapel-arch of a window, he can just see the treetops of Gordon Square, burnished with autumn, and far below, the gardeners raking leaves and lifting bulbs. Beyond it, from this height, he can see as far as Tavistock Square, though the old copper beech stands between him and a view of his own attic window at the top of Connaught Hall.

He tries not to think about Ella, whom he hopes to find, several hours from now, on the other side of that window, in his room – i.e., his bed – where they have agreed to meet to 'compare the findings' of their respective days. Ella, a literature student, has been coolly bluffing her way into the Press Box at The Old Bailey for the last week or so. For his part, he'd never heard of the infamous novel until the headlines got hold of it, but Ella is gripped and garrulous, and even the sound of her voice in his ear fills him with a desire worthy of the finest dirty book.

He paces, mug in hand. He can't bring himself to leave his fibres unattended while they heal.

He watches the clock.

He checks the fibres. Too soon.

He deposits his mug on the window sill and busies himself with his prep. He fills the first glass micro-pipette with potassium chloride, inserts the silver thread-wire and connects it to the valve on his home-made amp. The glass pipette in his hand always brings to mind the old wooden dibber, smooth with use, that his father used during spring planting. Denis can see him still, in his weekend pull-over and tie, on his knees in the garden, as he dibbed and dug for a victory that was in no hurry to come. Only his root vegetables ever rewarded his efforts.

Soon, Antony and Günter, his undergrad assistants, will shuffle in for duty. He'll post Antony, with the camera and a stockpile of film, at the oscilloscope's screen. Günter will take to the dark room next to the lab, and emerge pale and blinking at the end of the day.

Outside, the transistor radio and its owner take their leave. He drains his coffee, glances at the clock, and checks his nails for sheep's blood. How much longer? He allows himself to wander as far as the stairwell and back again. He doodles on the blackboard – a sickle moon, a tree, a stick man clinging to a branch – and erases all three.

At last, at last. He prepares a slide, sets up the Zeiss, switches on its light and swivels the lens into place. At this magnification, the fibre cells are pulsing minnows of life. His 'dibbers' are ready; Günter passes him the first and checks its connection to the amp. Denis squints over the Zeiss and inserts the micro–pipette into a cell membrane. The view is good. He can even spot the two boss–eyed nuclei. If the second pipette penetrates the cell successfully, he'll make contact with the innermost life of the cell.

His wrist is steady, which means every impulse, every rapid–fire excitation, should travel up the pipette through the thread–wire and into the valve of the amplifier. The oscilloscope will 'listen' to the amp. Fleeting waves of voltage will rise and fall across its screen, and Antony will snap away on the Nikon, capturing every fluctuation, every trace. Günter, for his part, has already removed himself like a penitent to the dark room. There, if all goes well, he'll capture the divine spark of life on Kodak paper, over and over again.

Later still, they'll convert the electrical ephemera of the day into scrolling graphs; they'll chart the unfolding peaks and troughs; they'll watch on paper the ineffable currents that compel the heart to life.

Cell after cell. Impulse upon impulse. An

ebb and flow of voltage. The unfolding story of a single heartbeat in thousandths of a second.

'Tell me,' says Ella, 'about your excitable cells. I like those.' Their heads share the one pillow. Schubert's piano trio is rising through the floorboards of the student hall. A cellist he has yet to meet lives below.

'I'll give you excitable.' He pinches her bottom. She bites the end of his nose. Through the crack of open window, they can smell trampled leaves, wet pavement and frost-bitten earth. In the night above the attic window, the stars throb.

She sighs luxuriously and shifts, so that Denis has to grip the mattress of the narrow single bed to steady himself. 'Excuse me, Miss, but I'm about to go over the edge.'

'Of the bed or your mental health? Have you found those canals yet?'

'Channels.'

'Precisely. Plutonium channels. See? I listen. You might not think I do, but I do.'

'Potassium. Potassium channels.'

'That's what I said.'

'I'm afraid you didn't. Which means…'

'Which means..?'

He rumples his brow in a display of forethought. 'Which means – and I say this with regret – I might just have to spank you.' He marvels at his own audacity. He is someone new with her and, at the same time, he has never felt more himself.

'Cheek!' she declares, and covers her own with the eiderdown. 'But I'm listening now. Tell me again. What do you do with these potassium channels?'

'I map their electrical activity. I demonstrate the movement of ions – electrically charged particles – through the cell membranes.' From the mattress edge, he gets a purchase by grabbing hold of her hip.

'Why aren't you more pleased?'

'Tell me about the trial today.'

'I thought you said those channels of yours were *the* challenge. The new discovery. The biologist's New World.'

'I'm pleased. Yes. Thanks. It's going well.' He throws back the eiderdown, springs to his feet and rifles through her shoulder bag for her notebook. 'Is it in here?'

'Is what?'

'Your notebook.'

'A man's testicles are never at their best as he bends,' she observes.

'So did The Wigs put on a good show today?'

She folds her arms across the eiderdown. 'I'm not talking dirty until you tell me about your potassium what-nots.'

'Channels.' From across the room, his back addresses her. 'They're simply passages or pores in the cell membrane that allow a mass of charged ions to be shunted into the cell – or out of it again if there's an excess.'

She sighs. 'If it's all so matter of fact, why are you bothering?'

He returns to her side, kisses the top of her head and negotiates his way back into the bed. 'My supervisor put me on the case, and, like I say, all's well. I'm getting the results, rather more quickly than I expected, so I'm pleased. Relieved even. Because in truth, I would have looked a little silly if I hadn't found them. They're already known to exist in muscle cells, and the heart is only another muscle after all.'

'Only another muscle?'

'Yes.' He flips through her notebook.

'But this is something that has you running through Bloomsbury in the middle of the night and leaving me for a date with a computer.'

He kisses her shoulder. 'The computer isn't nearly so amiable.'

'Denis Noble, are you doing interesting work or aren't you?'

'I have a dissertation to produce.'

'Please. Never be, you know…take it or leave it. Never be bored. Men who are bored bore me.'

'Then I shall stifle every yawn.'

'You'll have to do better than that. Tell me what you aim to discover next.' She divests him of his half of the eiderdown, and he grins, in spite of the cold.

'Whatever it is, you'll be the first to know.'

'Perhaps it isn't an "it",' she muses. 'Have you thought of that?'

'How can "it" not be an "it"?'

'I'm not sure,' she says, and she wraps herself up like the Queen of Sheba. The eiderdown crackles with static, and her fine, shiny hair flies away in the light of the desk-lamp. 'But a book, for example, is not an "it".'

'Of course it's an "it". It's an object, a thing. Ask any girl in her deportment class, as she walks about with one on her head.'

'Then I'll re-phrase, shall I? A story is not an "it". If it's any good, it's more alive than an "it". Every part of a great story "contains" every other part. Every small part anticipates the whole. Nothing can be passive or static. Nothing is just a part. Not really. Because the whole, if it's powerful enough that is, cannot be divided. That's what a great creation is. It has its own marvellous unity.' She pauses to examine the birthmark on his hip, a new discovery. 'Of course, I'm fully aware I sound like a) a girl and b) a dreamy arts student, but I suspect the heart *is* a great creation and that the same rule applies.'

'And which *rule* might that be?' He loves listening to her, even if he has no choice but to mock her, gently.

'The same principle then.'

He raises an eyebrow.

She adjusts her generous breasts. 'The principle of Eros. Eros is an attractive force. It binds the world; it makes connections. At best, it gives way to a sense of wholeness, a sense of the sacred even; at worst, it leads to fuzzy vision. Logos, your contender, particularises. It makes the elements of the world distinct. At best, it is illuminating; at worst, it is reductive. It cheapens. Both are vital. The balance is the thing. You need Eros, Denis. You're missing Eros.'

He passes her her notebook and taps it. 'On that point, we agree entirely. I wait with the utmost patience.'

She studies him with suspicion, then opens the spiral-bound stenographer's notebook. In the days before the trial, she taught herself shorthand in record time simply to capture, like any other putative member of the press, the banned passages of prose. She was determined to help carry their erotic charge into the world. 'T.S. Eliot was supposed to give evidence for the defense today, but apparently he sat in his taxi and couldn't bring himself to "do the deed".'

'Old men – impotent. Young men' – he smiles shyly and nods to his exposed self – 'ready.' He opens her notebook to a random page of shorthand. The ink is purple.

'My little joke,' she says. 'A sense of humour is *de rigueur* in the Press Box.' She nestles into the pillow and relinquishes his half of the eiderdown. He pats down her fly-away hair. 'From Chapter Ten,' she begins. '"Then with a quiver of exquisite pleasure he touched the warm soft body, and touched her navel for a moment in a kiss. And he had to come into her at once, to enter the peace on earth of her soft quiescent body. It was the moment of pure peace for him, the entry into the body of a woman.'"

'That gamekeeper chap doesn't hang about,' he says, his smile twitching.

'Quiet,' she chides. 'He is actually a very noble sort. Not sordid like you.'

'My birth certificate would assure you that I'm a Noble sort.'

'Ha ha.'

Denis lays his head against her breast and listens to the beat of her heart as she reads. Her voice enters him like a current and radiates through him until he feels himself almost hum with it, as if he is the body of a violin or cello that exists only to amplify her voice. He suspects he is not in love with her – and that is really just as well – but it occurs to him that he has never known such sweetness, such delight. He tries to stay in the moment, to loiter in the beats between the words she reads, between the breaths she takes. He runs his hand over the bell of her hip and tries not to think that in just four hours he will set off into the darkened streets of Bloomsbury, descend a set of basement steps and begin his night shift in the company of the only computer at the University of London that is powerful enough to crunch his milliseconds of data into readable equations.

As a lowly biologist, an ostensible lightweight

among the physicists and computer guys, he has been allocated the least enviable slot on the computer, from two till four am. By five, he'll be on the Northern Line again, heading for the slaughterhouse.

Ella half wakes as he leaves.

'Go back to sleep,' he whispers. He grabs his jacket and the hold-all.

She sits up in bed, blinking in the light of the lamp which he has turned to the wall. 'Are you going now?'

'Yes.' He smiles, glancing at her, finds his wallet and checks he has enough for the hearts of the day.

'Goodbye, Denis,' she says softly.

'Sweet dreams,' he says.

But she doesn't stretch and settle back under the eiderdown. She remains upright and naked even though the room is so cold, their breath has turned to frost on the inside of the window. He wonders if there isn't something odd in her expression. He hovers for a moment before deciding it is either a shadow from the lamp or the residue of a dream. Whatever the case, he can't be late for his shift. If he is, the porter in the unit won't be there to let him in – which means he has no more time to think on it.

He switches off the lamp.

In his later years, Denis Noble has allowed himself to wonder, privately, about the physiology of love. He has loved – with gratitude and frustration – parents, siblings, a spouse and two children. What, he asks himself, is love if not a force within? And what is a force within if not something *lived through* the body? Nevertheless, as Emeritus Professor of Cardiovascular Physiology, he has to admit he knows little more about love than he did on the night he fell in love with his mother; the night their shelter was bombed; the night he felt with utter certainty the strange and secret life of the heart within his chest.

Before 1960 drew to a close, he would – like hundreds of thousands of other liberated readers – buy the banned book and try to understand it as Ella had understood it. Later still in life, he would dedicate himself to the music and poetry of the Occitan troubadours. ('*I only know the grief that comes to me, to my love-ridden heart, out of over-loving…*') He would read and re-read the ancient sacred–sexual texts of the Far East. He would learn, almost by heart, St. Theresa's account of her vision of the seraph: '*I saw in his hands a long spear of gold, and at the iron's point there seemed to be a little fire. He appeared to me to be thrusting it at times into my heart, and to pierce my very entrails; when he drew it out, he seemed to draw them out also, and to leave me all on fire with a great love of God. The pain was so great that it made me moan; and yet so surpassing was the sweetness of this excessive pain that I could not wish to be rid of it.*'

But *what*, he wanted to ask St. Theresa, could

the heart, that feat of flesh, blood and voltage, have to do with love? *Where*, he'd like to know, is love? *How* is love?

On the train to Totteridge, he can still smell the citrus of Ella's perfume on his hands, in spite of all the punched paper-tape offerings he's been feeding to the computer through the night. He only left its subterranean den an hour ago. These days, the slots of his schedule are his daily commandments.

He is allowed 'to live' and to sleep from seven each evening to half past one the next morning, when his alarm wakes him for his shift in the computer unit. He closes the door on the darkness of Connaught Hall and sprints across Bloomsbury. After his shift, he travels from the Comp. Science basement to the Northern Line, from the Northern Line to the slaughterhouse, from the slaughterhouse to Euston, and from Euston to the lab for his twelve-hour day. 'Seven to seven,' he declares to his supervisor. He arrives home to Connaught Hall for supper at seven-thirty, Ella at eight, sleep at ten and three hours' oblivion until the alarm rings and the cycle starts all over again.

He revels briefly in the thought of a pretty girl still asleep in his bed, a luxury he'd never dared hope to win as a science student. Through the smeared carriage windows, the darkness is thinning into a murky dawn. The Thermos jiggles in the hold-all at his feet, the carriage door rattles and clangs, and his head falls back.

Up ahead, Ella is standing naked and grand on a bright woodland path in Tavistock Square. She doesn't seem to care that she can be seen by all the morning commuters and the students rushing past on their way to classes. She slips through the gate at the western end of the square and turns, closing it quickly. As he reaches it, he realises it is a kissing-gate. She stands on the other side but refuses him her lips. 'Gates open,' she says tenderly, 'and they close.' He tries to go through but she shakes her head. When he pulls on the gate, he gets an electric shock. 'Why are you surprised?' she says. Then she's disappearing through another gate into Gordon Square, and her hair is flying-away in the morning light, as if she herself is electric. He pulls again on the gate, but it's rigid.

The dream returns to him only later as Marty is scooping the pluck from the first sheep on the line.

He feels again the force of that electric shock.

The gate was conductive...

It opened... It closed.

It *closed*.

He receives from Marty the first heart of the day. It's hot between his palms but he doesn't reach for his scissors. He doesn't open the Thermos. He hardly moves. Deep within him, it's as if his own heart has been jump-started to life.

In the operating theatre, Mr Bonham and his team have been at work for three-and-a-half hours, when at last he gives the word. Professor Noble can be disconnected from the bypass machine. His pulse is strong. The new heart, declares Mr Bonham, 'is going great guns'.

His dream of Ella at the gate means he can't finish at the slaughterhouse quickly enough. On the train back into town, he swears under his breath at the eternity of every stop. In the lab, he wonders if the ends of the Purkinje fibres will ever close and heal. He has twelve hours of lab time. Seven to seven. Will it be enough?

Twelve hours pass like two. The fibres are tricky today. He botched more than a few in the dissection, and the insertion of the micro-pipette has been hit and miss. Antony and Günter exchange looks. They discover he has amassed untold quantities of film, and he tells Antony he wants a faster shutter speed. When they request a lunch break, he simply stares into the middle distance. When Günter complains that his hands are starting to burn from the fixatives, Denis looks up from his micro-pipette, as if at a tourist who requires something of him in another language.

Finally, when the great window is a chapel arch of darkness and rain, he closes and locks the lab door behind him. There is nothing in his appearance to suggest anything other than a long day's work. No one he passes on the grand staircase of the Anatomy Building pauses to look. No one glances back, pricked by an intuition or an after-thought. He has remembered his hold-all and the Thermos for tomorrow's hearts. He has forgotten his jacket, but the sight of a poorly dressed student is nothing to make anyone look twice.

Yet as he steps into the downpour of the night, every light is blazing in his head. His brain is Piccadilly Circus, and in the dazzle, he hardly sees where he's going but he's running, across Gordon Square and on towards Tavistock... He wants to shout the news to the winos who shelter from the rain under dripping trees. He wants to holler it to every lit window, to every student in his or her numinous haze of thought. He wants to dash up the stairs of Connaught Hall, knock on the door of the mystery cellist, and blurt out the words. Tomorrow at the slaughterhouse, he tells himself, he might even have to hug Marty and Alf. 'They *close!*'

He saw it with his own eyes: potassium channels that *closed*.

They did just the opposite of what everyone expected.

He assumed some sort of experimental error. He went back through Günter's contact sheets. He checked the amp and the connections. He wondered if he wasn't merely observing his own wishful thinking. He started again. He shook things up. He subjected the cells to change – changes of voltage, of ions, of temperature. Antony asked, morosely, for permission to leave early. He had an exam – Gross Anatomy – the next day. Didn't Antony understand? 'They're not simply open,' he announced over a new ten-pound cylinder of graph paper. 'They *opened*.'

Antony's face was blank as an egg.

Günter suggested they call it a day.

But the channels opened. They were active. They opened *and*, more remarkably still, they *closed*.

Ella was right. He'll tell her she was. He'll be the first to admit it. The channels aren't merely passive conduits. They're not just machinery or component parts. They're alive and responsive.

Too many ions inside the cell – too much stress, exercise, anger, love, lust or despair – and they close. They stop all incoming electrical traffic. They preserve calm in the midst of too much life. They allow the ion gradient to stabilise.

He can hardly believe it himself. The heart 'listens' to itself. Causation isn't just upward; it's unequivocally downward too. It's a beautiful loop of feedback. The parts of the heart listen to each other as surely as musicians in an ensemble listen to each other. That's what he's longing to tell Ella. *That's* what he's discovered. Forget the ensemble. The heart is an *orchestra*. It's the BBC Proms. It's the Boston Pops. Even if he only understands its rhythm section today, he knows this now. The heart is infinitely more than the sum of its parts.

And he can prove it mathematically. The super computer will vouch for him, he feels sure of it. He'll design the equations. He'll come up with a computer model that will make even the physicists and computer scientists stand and gawp.

Which is when it occurs to him: what if the heart doesn't stop at the heart? What if the connections don't end?

Even he doesn't quite know what he means by this.

He will ask Ella. He will tell her of their meeting at the kissing-gate. He will ask for the kiss her dream-self refused him this morning. He'll enjoy the sweet confusion on her face.

Ella at eight.

Ella always at eight.

He waits by the window until the lights go out over Tavistock Square and the trees melt into darkness.

He waits for three days. He retreats under the eiderdown. He is absent from the slaughterhouse, the lab and the basement.

A fortnight passes. A month. The new year.

When the second movement of the Piano Trio rises through the floorboards, he feels nothing. It has taken him months, but finally, he feels nothing.

As he comes round, the insult of the tube down his throat assures him he hasn't died.

The first thing he sees is his grandson by the

foot of his bed tapping away on his new mobile phone. 'Hi Granddad,' Josh says, as if Denis has only been napping. He bounces to the side of the ICU bed, unfazed by the bleeping monitors and the tubes. 'Put your index finger here, Denis. I'll help you... No, like right *over* the camera lens. That's it. This phone has an Instant Heart Rate App. We'll see if you're working yet.'

'Cool,' Denis starts to say, but the irony is lost to the tube in his throat.

Josh's brow furrows. He studies his phone screen like a doctor on a medical soap. 'Sixty-two beats per minute at rest. Congratulations, Granddad. You're like...alive.' Josh squeezes his hand and grins.

Denis has never been so glad to see him.

On the other side of the bed, his wife touches his shoulder. Her face is tired. The fluorescence of the lights age her. She has lipstick on her front tooth and tears in her eyes as she bends to whisper, hoarsely, in his ear. 'You came back to me.'

The old words.

After a week, he'd given up hope. He realised he didn't even know where she lived, which student residence, which flat, which telephone exchange. He'd never thought to ask. Once he even tried waiting for her outside The Old Bailey, but the trial was over, someone told him. Days before. Didn't he read the papers?

When she opened his door in January of '61, she stood on the threshold, like an apparition who might at any moment disappear again. She simply waited, her shiny hair still flying away from her in the light of the bare bulb on the landing. He was standing at the window through which he'd given up looking. On the other side, the copper beech was bare with winter. In the room below, the Schubert recording was stuck on a scratch.

Her words, when they finally came, were hushed and angry. They rose and fell in a rhythm he'd almost forgotten. 'Why don't you *know* that you're in love with me? What's wrong with you, Denis Noble?'

Cooking smells – boiled vegetables and mince – wafted into his room from the communal kitchen on the floor below. It seemed impossible that she should be here. Ella. Not Ella at eight. *Ella.*

Downstairs, the cellist moved the needle on the record.

'You came back to me,' he said.

His eyes filled.

*

As his recuperation begins, he will realise, with not a little impatience, that he knows nothing at all about the whereabouts of love. He knows only where it isn't. It is not in the heart, or if it is, it is not only in the heart. The organ that first beat in the depths of Ethel in the upstairs room of Wilson & Jeffries is now consigned to the scrap-heap of cardiovascular history. Yet in this moment, with a heart that is not strictly his, he loves Ella as powerfully as he did the night she re-appeared in his room on Tavistock Square.

But if love is not confined to the heart, nor would it seem is memory confined to the brain. The notion tantalises him. Those aspects or qualities which make the human condition human – love, consciousness, memory, affinity – are, Denis feels more sure than ever, *distributed* throughout the body. The single part, as Ella once claimed so long ago, must contain the whole.

He hopes his new heart will let him live long enough to see the proof. He'll have to chivvy the good folk at the Physiome Project along.

He wishes he had a pencil.

In the meantime, as Denis adjusts to his new heart hour by hour, day by day, he will demonstrate, in Josh's steadfast company, an imperfect but unprecedented knowledge of the lyrics of Jay-Z and OutKast. He will announce to Ella that he is keen to buy a BMX bike. He won't be sure himself whether he is joking or not. He will develop an embarrassing appetite for doner kebabs, and he will not be deterred by the argument, put to him by Ella, his daughter and Josh, that he has never eaten a doner kebab in his entire life.

He will surprise even himself when he hears himself tell Mr Bonham, during his evening rounds, that he favours Alton Towers over the Dordogne this year.

Wires

Jon McGregor

IT WAS A sugar-beet, presumably, since that was
a sugar-beet lorry in front of her and this thing
turning in the air at something like sixty miles
an hour had just fallen off it. It looked sort of
like a giant turnip, and was covered in mud, and
basically looked more or less like whatever she
would have imagined a sugar-beet to look like if
she'd given it any thought before now. Which she
didn't think she had. It was totally filthy. They
didn't make sugar out of that, did they? What did
they do, grind it? Cook it?

Regardless, whatever, it was coming straight
for her.

Meaning this was, what, one of those time-
slows-down moments or something. Her life was
presumably going to start flashing in front of her
eyes right about now. She wondered why she
hadn't screamed or anything. 'Oh,' seemed to
be about as much as she'd managed. But in the
time it had taken to say 'Oh,' she'd apparently

had the time to make a list of all the things she
was having the time to think about, like, i.e.,
Item One, how she'd said 'Oh' without any panic
or fear, and did that mean she was repressed or
just calm or collected or what; *Item Two*, what
would Marcus say when he found out, would he
try and find someone to blame, such as herself for
driving too close or even for driving on her own
at all, or such as the lorry driver for overloading
the lorry, or such as her, again, for not having
joined the union like he'd told her to, like anyone
was in a union these days, especially anyone
with a part-time job who was still at uni and not
actually all that bothered about pension rights or
legal representation; *Item Three*, but she couldn't
possibly be thinking all this in the time it was
taking for the sugar-beet to turn in the air and
crash through the windscreen, if that's what it was
going to do, and what then, meaning this must be
like a neural-pathway illusion or something; *Item
Four*, actually Marcus did go on sometimes, he
did reckon himself, and how come she thought
things like that about him so often, maybe she was
being unfair, because they were good together,
people had told her they were good together, but
basically she was confused and she didn't know
where she stood; *Item Five*, a witty and deadpan
way of mentioning this on her status update would
be something like, Emily Wilkinson is sweet
enough already thanks without a sugar-beet in the
face, although actually she wouldn't be able to put

that, if that's what was actually going to happen, thinking about it logically; *Item Six*, although did she really even know what a neural-pathway was, or was it just something she'd heard someone else talk about and decided to start saying?

Item Seven was just, basically, wtf.

Meanwhile: before she had time to do anything useful, like e.g. swerve or brake or duck or throw her arms up in front of her face, the sugar-beet smashed through the windscreen and thumped into the passenger seat beside her. There was a roar of cold air. And now she swerved, only now, once there was no need and it just made things more dangerous, into the middle lane and back again into the slow lane. It was totally instinctive, and totally useless, and basically made her think of her great-grandad saying God help us if there's a war on. She saw other people looking at her, or she thought she did, all shocked faces and big mouths; a woman pulling at her boyfriend's arm and pointing, a man swearing and reaching for his phone, another man in a blue van waving her over to the hard shoulder. But she might have imagined this, or invented it afterwards. Marcus was always saying that people didn't look at her as much as she thought they did. She never knew whether he meant this to reassure her or if he was saying she reckoned herself too much.

Anyway. Point being. Status update: Emily Wilkinson is still alive.

She pulled over to the hard shoulder and came to a stop. The blue van pulled over in front of her. She put her hazard lights on and listened to the clicking sound they made. When she looked up the people in the passing cars already had no idea what had happened. The drama was over. The traffic was back to full speed, the lorry was already miles down the road. She wondered if she was supposed to start crying. She didn't feel like crying.

Someone was standing next to the car. 'Bloody hell,' he said. He peered in at her through the hole in the windscreen. He looked like a mechanic or a breakdown man or something. He was wearing a waxed jacket with rips in the elbows, and jeans. He looked tired; his eyes were puffy and dark and his breathing was heavy. He rested his hand on the bonnet and leaned in closer. 'Bloody *hell*,' he said again, raising his voice against the traffic; 'you all right, love?' She smiled, and nodded, and shrugged, which was weird, which meant was she for some reason apologising for his concern? '*Bloody* hell,' he said for a third time. 'You could have been killed.'

Thanks. Great. This was, what, news?

She looked down at the sugar-beet, which was sitting on a heap of glass on the passenger seat beside her. The bits of glass were small and lumpy, like gravel. She noticed more bits of glass on the floor, and the dashboard, and spread across her lap.

She noticed that her left arm was scratched, and
that she was still holding on to the steering wheel,
and that maybe she wasn't breathing quite as much
as she should have been, although that happened
whenever she thought about her breathing, it
going wrong like that, too deep or too shallow
or too quick, although that wasn't just her
though, surely, it was one of those well-known
paradoxes, like a Buddhist thing or something:
total mindlessness, or mindfulness. Just breathe.

'The police are on their way,' someone
else said. She looked up and saw another man, a
younger man in a sweatshirt and jeans, holding up
a silver phone. 'I just called the police,' he said.
'They're on their way.' He seemed pleased to
have a phone with him, the way he was holding
it, like this was his first one or something. Which
there was no way. His jeans had grass-stains on the
knees, and his boots were thick with mud.

'You called them, did you?' the older man
asked. The younger man nodded, and put his
phone in his pocket, and looked at her. She sat
there, waiting for the two of them to catch up.
Like; yes, a sugar-beet had come through the
windscreen; no, she wasn't hurt; yes, this other
guy did phone the police. Any further questions? I
can email you the notes? The younger man looked
through the hole in the windscreen, and at the
windscreen itself, and whistled. Actually whistled:
this long descending note like the sound-effect of
a rock falling towards someone's head in an old

film. What was that?

'You all right?' he asked her. 'You cut or anything? You in shock?' She shook her head. Not that she knew how she would know she was in shock. She was pretty sure one of the symptoms of being in shock would be not thinking you were in shock. Like with hypothermia, when you take off your clothes and roll around laughing in the snow. She'd read that somewhere. He looked at the sugar-beet and whistled again. 'I mean,' he said, and now she didn't know if he was talking to her or to the other man; 'that could've been fatal, couldn't it?' The other man nodded and said something in agreement. They both looked at her again. 'You could have been killed,' the younger man said. It was good of him to clarify that for her. She wondered what she was supposed to say. They looked as if they were waiting for her to ask something, to ask for help in some way.

'Well. Thanks for stopping,' she said. They could probably go now, really, if they'd called the police. There was no need to wait. She thought she probably wanted them to go now.

'Oh no, it's nothing, don't be daft,' the older man said.

'Couldn't just leave you like that, could we?' the younger man said. He looked at her arm. 'You're bleeding,' he said. 'Look.' He pointed to the scratches on her arm, and she looked down at herself. She could see the blood, but she couldn't feel anything. There wasn't much of it. It could be someone else's, couldn't it? But there wasn't anyone else. It must be hers. But she couldn't feel anything. She looked back at the younger man.

'It's fine,' she said. 'It's nothing. Really. Thanks.'

'No, it might be though,' he said, 'it might get infected. You have to be careful with things like that. There's a first-aid box in the van. Hang on.' He turned and walked back to the van, a blue Transit with the name and number of a landscape gardening company painted across the back, and a little cartoon gardener with a speech bubble saying no job was too small. The doors were tied shut with a length of orange rope. The number-plate was splattered with mud, but it looked like a K-reg. K450 something, although she wasn't sure if that was 0 the number or O the letter. The older man turned and smiled at her, while they were waiting, and she supposed that was him trying to be reassuring but to be honest it looked a bit weird. Although he probably couldn't help it. He probably had some kind of condition. Like a degenerative eye condition, maybe? And then on top of that, which would be painful enough, he had to put up with people like her thinking he looked creepy when he was just trying to be nice. She smiled back; she didn't want him thinking she'd been thinking all that about him looking creepy or weird.

'Police will be here in a minute,' he said. She nodded. 'Lorry must have been overloaded,' he said. 'Driver's probably none the wiser even now.'

'No,' she said, glancing down at the sugar-beet again. 'I suppose not.' The younger man came back, waving a green plastic first-aid box at her. He looked just as pleased as when he'd held up the phone. She wondered if he was on some sort of special supported apprenticeship or something, if he was a little bit learning-challenged, and then she thought it was probably discriminatory of her to have even thought that and she tried to get the thought out of her mind. Only you can't get thoughts out of your mind just by trying; that was another one of those Buddhist things. She should just concentrate on not thinking about her breathing instead, she thought. Just, total mindlessness. Mindfulness. Just breathe.

He passed the first-aid box through the hole in the windscreen. His hands were stained with oil and mud, and as they touched hers they felt heavy and awkward. She put the box in her lap and opened it. She wondered what he wanted her to do. 'I don't know,' he said. 'I just thought. Has it got antiseptic cream in there?' She rummaged through the bandages and wipes and creams and scissors. And now what. She took out a wipe, dabbed at her arm, and closed the box. She handed it back to him, holding the bloody wipe in one hand.

'Thanks,' she said. 'I think I'll be okay now.' Was she talking too slowly? Patronising him?

Or was she making reasonable allowances for his learning-challenges? But he might not even be that. She was over-complicating the situation, probably. Which was another thing Marcus said to her sometimes, that she did that. She looked at him. He shrugged.

'Well, yeah,' he said. 'If you're sure. I just thought, you know.'

Status update: Emily Wilkinson regrets not having signed up for breakdown insurance.

'Thanks,' she said.

She'd chosen Hull because she'd thought it would sound interesting to say she was going to a provincial university. Or more exactly because she thought it would make her sound interesting to even say 'provincial university', which she didn't think anyone had said since about 1987 or some other time way before she was born. She wasn't even exactly sure what provincial meant. Was it just anywhere not-London? That seemed pretty sweeping. That was where most people lived. Maybe it meant anywhere that wasn't London or Oxford or Cambridge, and that was still pretty sweeping. Whatever, people didn't seem to say it anymore, which was why she'd been looking forward to saying it. Only it turned out that no one knew what she was talking about and they mostly thought she was saying provisional, which totally wasn't the same thing at all.

Anyway though, that hadn't been the only

reason she'd chosen Hull. Another reason was it was a long way from home. As in definitely too far to visit. Plus when she went on the open day she'd loved the way the river smelt of the sea, and obviously the bridge, which looked like something from a film, and also the silence you hit when you got to the edge of the town, and the way it didn't take long to get to the edge of town. And of course she'd liked the Larkin thing, except again it didn't seem like too many people were bothered about that. Or knew about it. Or knew how much it meant, if they did know about it. When she first got there she kept putting 'Emily Wilkinson is a bit chilly and smells of fish' on her status updates, but no one got the reference so she gave it up. Plus it made her look weird, obviously, even after she'd explained it in the comments.

She'd met Marcus in her second year, when he'd taught a module on 'The Literature of Marginal(ised) Places'. Which she'd enjoyed enough to actually go to at least half of the lectures rather than just collect the notes. He had a way of explaining things like he properly wanted you to understand, instead of just wanting to show off or get through the class as quick as he could. There was something sort of generous about the way he talked, in class, and the way he listened to the students. Plus he was what it was difficult to think of a better word for than totally buff, and also had what she couldn't be more articulate than call a lovely mouth, and basically made her spend quite a lot of time not actively addressing the issues of appropriation inherent in a socially dominant form such as literary fiction taking exclusion and marginality as its subject. Her friend Jenny had said she couldn't see it at all, as in the buffness and the lovely mouth rather than the inherent appropriation, but that had only made her think it was maybe something more along the lines of a genuine connection thing and not just some kind of stereotypical type of crush; and Jenny did at least agree that no way did it count as inappropriate if it was just a PhD student and not an actual lecturer. His last seminar had been on the Tasmanian novel, which it turned out there were quite a few of, and afterwards he'd kept her talking until the others had left and said were there any issues she wanted to discuss and actually did she want to go for a drink. To which her response had been, And that took you so long why?

There hadn't really been anyone before Marcus. Not since coming to university, anyway. There'd been a few things at parties, and she'd slept with one of her housemates a bunch of times, but nothing serious enough to make her change her relationship setting. With Marcus it had been different, almost immediately. He'd asked her out, like formally, and they'd had late-night conversations about their relationship and what relationships meant and even whether or not they were in love and how they would know and whether love could ever be defined without reference to the other. She didn't really know. She thought being in love probably didn't mean telling your girlfriend what she could wear when you went to the pub together, or asking her not to talk to certain people, or telling her she was the reason you couldn't finish your thesis.

They hadn't moved in together, but almost as soon as they'd started going out their possessions had begun drifting from one house to the other until it felt like they were just living together in two places. Sometimes when she woke up it took her a moment to remember which house she was in. It wasn't always a nice feeling. Which meant, what? She fully had no idea what it meant. Because she liked Marcus, she liked him a lot. She liked the conversations they had, which were smart and complicated and went on for hours. And she liked the way he looked at her when he wanted to do the things she'd been thinking about in class when she should have been thinking about discourses of liminality, when she'd been imagining saying he was welcome to cross her threshold any day. There was still all that. But there were other things. Things that made her uncomfortable, uncertain, things she was pretty sure weren't part of how a relationship was supposed to make you feel happy or good about yourself or whatever it was a relationship was supposed to make you feel.

She should be calling him now, and she wasn't. He'd want her to have called, when he heard. Something like this. He should be the first person she thought of calling. He'd think it was odd that she hadn't. He'd be hurt. She thought about calling Jenny instead, to tell her what had happened, or her supervisor, to tell her she'd be late getting back to the office. She should call someone, probably, but she couldn't really imagine having the words to explain it and she couldn't face having anyone else tell her she could have been killed and plus anyway she was totally fine, wasn't she? She looked down at the sugar-beet again. Was that what that smell was? It wasn't a sugary smell at all. It was more like an earthy smell, like wet earth, like something rotting in the earth. She didn't see how they could get from that to a bowl of white sugar on a café table, or even to that sort of wet, boozy smell you got when you drove past the refinery, coming up the A1. Which come to think of it was probably where the lorry would have been heading. It would be, what, an hour's drive from here? Maybe she should go there and give them back their sugar-beet, tell them what had happened. Complain, maybe.

The passenger door opened, and the older man leaned in towards her.

'You need to get out,' he said. It seemed a bit too directive, the way he said it. She didn't move. 'It's not safe, being on the hard shoulder like this,' he added. 'We should all be behind the barrier.' They'd been discussing this, had they?

It looked like they'd been discussing something. The older man was already holding out his hand to help her across the passenger seat. She looked at the traffic, roaring and weaving and hurtling past, and she remembered hearing about incidents where people had been struck and killed on the hard shoulder, when they were changing a tyre, or going for a piss, or just stopping to help. She remembered her cousin once telling her about a school minibus which had driven into the back of a Highways Maintenance truck and burst into flames. Which meant they were right about this, did it, probably? She swung her feet over into the passenger's side, took the man's hand, and squeezed out on to the tarmac. It was an awkward manoeuvre, and she didn't think she'd completed it with much elegance or style. The younger man was already standing behind the barrier, and she clambered over to join him. She didn't do that very gracefully either. He started climbing up the embankment.

'Just in case,' he said, looking back at her. Meaning what, she wondered. 'Something could flip, couldn't it?' he said, and he did something with his hands which was presumably supposed to look like a vehicle striking a barrier and somersaulting across it. The older man caught her eye, and nodded, and she followed them both up the embankment, through the litter and the long grass.

It was much colder at the top. Sort of exposed.

The wind was whipping away the sound of the traffic, making her feel further from the road than they really were. The two men looked awkward, as though maybe they were uncomfortable about the time this whole situation was taking. The younger man made the whistling noise again. She could barely hear it against the wind.

'You're lucky,' he said, nodding down towards her car. 'I mean, you know. You're lucky we stopped. You could have been killed.' She didn't know what to say to this. She nodded, and folded her arms against the cold. The older man arched his back, rubbing at his neck with both hands.

'They'll be here soon,' he said, and she nodded again, looking around.

Behind them, the ground sloped away towards a small woodland of what she thought might be hawthorn or rowan trees or something like that. The ones with the red berries. There were ragged strips of bin-liners and carrier-bags hanging from the branches, flapping in the wind. Past the trees, there was a warehouse, and an access road, and she noticed that the streetlights along the access road were coming on already. Beyond the access road, a few miles further away, there were some houses which she wasn't sure if they were some estate on the outskirts of Hull or some other town altogether. Hull was further than that, she was pretty sure. It was the other side of the estuary, and they were still south of the river.

Almost certainly.

The older man started down the slope, towards the trees. 'I'm just going to, you know,' he said. 'While we're waiting.' She turned away, looking back at the road. She was getting colder now. She looked at her car, and at the blue van. They were both rocking gently in the slipstream of the passing traffic, their hazard lights blinking in sequence. She wondered if she felt like crying yet. She didn't think so. It still didn't seem like the right moment.

She would talk to Marcus at the weekend, she decided. He'd understand, when it came down to it. Once he gave her a chance to explain. She'd say something like although they'd been good together at times and she was still very fond of him she just couldn't see where things were going for them. She didn't like the way he made her feel about herself, sometimes. She needed some time to find out who she was and what she needed from a relationship. Something like that.

She'd tried it out with Jenny. Jenny had said it sounded about right. Jenny had said she thought Marcus was reasonable and would probably take it on board, although obviously he'd still be disappointed. That was how she talked sometimes, like she was a personal guidance counsellor or something, or an older and wiser cousin. Whereas in fact she was only like a year older, and had spent that year mostly in Thailand and Australia, which was her version of travelling the world and which she thought made her the total source of wisdom when in fact it made her the total source of knowing about youth hostels and full-moon parties and not even having heard of Philip fucking Larkin. And she was wrong about Marcus. It was way more likely he would shout at her when she told him. Or break something. It wouldn't be the first time. Everyone thought he was so reasonable. But she wasn't going to back down this time. She was certain of it, suddenly. Something like this, it made you think about things, about your priorities. She could say that to him, in fact. She could explain what had happened and that it had made her rethink a few things. Maybe she should call him now in fact, and tell him what had happened. So he'd already have the context when she talked about wanting to finish things. Maybe that would be sensible. She should do that. She wanted to do that, she realised. She wanted to hear his voice, and to know that he knew she was okay. Which meant what. She wanted him to know where she was. Her phone was still in her bag, in the car. She started to move down the embankment. The younger man grabbed her arm.

'You should stay up here,' he said. 'It's safer.' She looked at him, and at his hand on her arm. 'They'll be here in a minute,' he said.

'I just need to get my phone,' she said. 'I need to call someone. I'll be careful, thanks.' She tried to step away, but he held her back. 'Excuse me?' she said.

'You're probably in shock,' he said. 'You should be careful. Maybe you should sit down.'

'I'm okay, actually, thanks? I don't want to sit down?' She spoke clearly, looking him in the eye, raising her voice above the wind and the traffic. Plus raising her voice against maybe he was a bit deaf, as well as the learning-challenged thing. She wanted him to let go of her arm. She tried to pull away again, but his grip was too tight. She looked at him, like: what are you doing? He shook his head. He said something else, but she couldn't hear him. She didn't know if the wind had picked up or what was going on. He looked confused, as if he couldn't remember what he was supposed to be saying.

She glanced down the other side of the embankment, and saw the older man at the edge of the woodland. He was standing with his back to the trees, looking up at the two of them, his hands held tensely by his sides. What was he. He seemed to be trying to say something to the younger man. He seemed to be waiting for something. She tried to pull away. But what.

The Human Circadian Pacemaker

K.J. Orr

HER FIRST GLIMPSE of him, he was walking towards
her lurching from side to side like a drunk. She
flung her arms around him.

'How are you?' she said.

A lop-sided smile. 'I'm A-OK.'

'So what have you been up to?'

'Stuff,' he said. 'You?'

'Oh, stuff.'

They didn't get to talk very much at first there was
so much going on. She went back home; he stayed
on for medical assessments, press conferences.

The first champagne reception she went to in
a dress she had bought for the occasion. Putting
it on she felt strangely like a schoolgirl going on
a date. She didn't know what he would be like
now, when so much had happened to him. Before
going out she threw a wrap over her shoulders

and then hugged herself in front of the mirror. He hadn't been home yet. Everything looked as it had for the last few months.

She had been warned, of course. Partners, spouses, went through training as well. They were told to expect change. They were warned about the psychological, the physiological. As they sat there on their chairs together in that room they had exchanged tentative smiles. Oh my goodness, their smiles said. What have we gotten ourselves into?

Sometimes at night she would lie in bed and run through the changes they had been told about and imagine the most extreme scenarios and be afraid. She would worry that he would come back with another man's face.

Arriving at the reception she waited for him to notice her standing on the parquet in her new dress, and he did notice her, and he walked over with his new rolling gait and he held on to her upper arms tight with his hands and looked at her.

'Hey,' she said.

'Hey yourself.'

His eyes were full of light. He looked giddy.

'Stay right where you are,' he said.

She watched him cross the floor to the long table where they were serving drinks. He collected two glasses of champagne, put them down to shake hands with the bartender, who looked pretty happy himself, picked them up again, wheeled around, and made his way back to her. He was finding his sea legs, walking on a shifting deck.

They had been warned about balance disorders, about hand-eye-head coordination, about posture, about gait, and she was glad they had been prepared, but annoyed now that she found herself watching him so closely, watching for the signs. It doesn't matter, she reminded herself. It won't last.

'You walk like a drunk,' she said, when he arrived, toppling, in front of her. He leaned towards her. She thought he was going to kiss her but he didn't. He raised the two glasses of champagne and looked at her over the small golden explosions.

She took her glass and they sipped at their champagne without speaking. It was cold and good. She didn't try to chink glasses: something might go wrong; hand-eye-head.

As the room filled, its constellations shifted between team clusters and family clusters. She watched and was glad that it had gone so well. She couldn't help studying the way he moved, gesticulated, the expressions that passed across his face. Even deep in conversation she listened out for him, weighed him up next to the others on some behavioural scale. A few of them were hamming it up, staggering about. One was rocking slowly backwards and forwards on the balls of his feet.

There were impromptu speeches, some of them quite silly. The team aired mission jokes which meant little to anyone else. A multitude of looks, smiles, gestures passed back and forth between them. It was like they shared some secret. Sometimes just glancing at each other would set them off.

In the faces of the other wives she recognized her own bewilderment.

They left the party about eleven; they sent them home, the team, like they were still in high school. They were told to get a good night's rest. Everyone shook hands. There were sparks of laughter. Manly hugs. Back patting. They all left the room together, everyone grinning and looking tired.

She drove home. He sat in the passenger seat across from her, his head lolling as they hit the dirt road; otherwise still, eyes shut.

The night was clear and she thought you must be able to see all of the stars. She wanted to pull over and get out of the car. She wanted to ask him – out in the middle of nowhere, by themselves – what it was like up there.

Tell me, she wanted to say, now that you're back – does space really smell like rubber? They say it does.

She thought about putting the radio on, but worried that the noise would wake him, so steering with one hand she wound down the window and pulled out her pack of cigarettes. When she had one lit she looked across at him, and then kept glancing back, every few seconds, all the way home.

They had been warned too about accelerated aging, cardiovascular de-conditioning, weakening of the muscles and bones, depressed immune response, disturbed sleep. None of them looked any older, but inside things had changed.

The human circadian pacemaker for one had undergone change. His rhythms were all off. His body clock was shot.

She woke to find him gone from their bed and there he was, sitting in the kitchen, three in the morning, looking at his hands.

'OK?' she said.

He looked up, but said nothing. She had the odd sensation that he didn't recognize her at all.

Before the mission the astronauts had used bright light to prepare for the flight, to help reset the body clock.

She had got a light box for his return. She had put it in the corner of their room, experimented with levels. At the highest it emitted a shock of bright white light that made her squint.

She pulled out a chair and sat across from him with a book. She had started it that week – though with the excitement of his return hadn't made much progress.

Now, under the disc of light cast by the lamp above them, she read.

At some point he got up and left the room. He got out of his chair so slowly she barely registered the movement. He walked like an old man. She moved to help but he waved her away, he said, 'I have to do this myself.' So she watched until he reached the doorway and turned to go upstairs, and then listened as he made his way one step at a time to the top.

She continued to read, as if the act, so far through the night and into the morning, were a way of keeping him company as he suffered under gravity.

They had regimes to keep them in shape. There were exercises to help maintain a basic level of health. The mission had been a long one though, and under the conditions there were limits to what a man could do. There were limits also to what he could control – certain things just happened. He had sent her a photo of himself with his 'space face'. He was all puffed up, they told her, due to a shift of fluids with the loss of gravity.

The night before launch he had been at the base. She had tried to sleep, but failed, and got up early. She opened the curtains and looked up at the sky, which was a perfect blue, just as it should be. She remembered a feeling of sawdust in her eyes, the sense she wasn't quite in her body.

So long as I don't have to talk to anyone, she thought. So long as I don't have to open my mouth.

When she got home she went straight to bed though it was still early. Lying on her side, she brought her knees up close to her chest and then wrapped one arm around them to pull them closer still. She tucked her other arm underneath the pillow. There her fingers found a packet of freeze-dried Neapolitan ice-cream. On the front, an image of a rocket launching into space; above it the words 'SPACE FOOD'. She had started laughing, and then she had found that she was crying instead.

With only one packet, she had been superstitious about using it. For weeks she carried it around like a charm. If she left the house without it she would go back and start her journey over. In time she discovered he'd hidden packets all over the place – slipped into socks in her underwear drawer, stowed inside DVD cases – so she no longer felt she always had to carry it around, and actually, finally, opened a packet to try it out. The taste wasn't bad, though the consistency was wrong. She wondered if this really was the stuff they had up there. She imagined them all opening and mixing their packets, discussing the flavours. There was something about it that made her laugh, the idea of them tearing open these things marked 'SPACE FOOD', as if they might go astray and eat the wrong kind of food without that heading in bold type to keep things clear.

She found no way to make space familiar, beyond this. She couldn't get past something imagined from childhood – tin cans; the Clangers; egg boxes with antennae made of flexible straws.

Upstairs, in their bedroom, the light box was brightening in the corner. It was domed, sun-like and set to progress through a simulated sunrise. He was balled up hidden beneath the duvet. She sat on the edge of the bed with his coffee in her hand and watched the light shift from red through orange to white.

She had met him at a small aerodrome in Texas. She was visiting a friend who was studying for a Ph.D. and who with time on her hands was considering taking flying lessons. They had gone along to watch the small training planes take off and land, over and over, on the thin strip of tarmac in the middle of all that dry earth. They sat in the heat drinking Coke, trying to make out faces in the stream of tiny planes. Each touched down for a moment only before taking off and looping around again. It was hypnotic enough and they were lazy enough to sit there until the circuits were over and the pilots and pupils came in and debriefed.

She had gone inside the hangar to use the toilet and was on her way out when she bumped into him. She was wiping her hands on her jeans, not looking where she was going. She recognized him as one of the pilots, and told him about her friend, and he had come to join them for a beer.

The three of them sat there until dark. Small planes appeared intermittently up above, lights winking like fireflies before touching down.

Late on, when her friend had gone inside, and they found themselves suddenly alone, something happened, there was an exchange of some sort, and awareness crept to the surface as they spoke, sitting there on aluminium chairs, their forearms resting on the cool table top.

He had come around, and stood behind her chair, lightly touched the back of her neck.

★

'I feel like shit,' he announced brightly, walking into the kitchen late morning, his eyes puffed up, blinking. 'I keep bumping into things,' he said. 'I hit my shin.' He showed her his leg. It was bleeding. Still, he was smiling.

'God,' she said. She took him in.

He asked for Marmite on toast. For someone who thought Marmite was a big joke he ate a lot of it. Her mother sent it over in packages from England. She hadn't told her that everything, now, you could get in the States. She liked receiving packages from her mother.

She asked him how long it would take for his body to adapt and he said he didn't know. Some people adapt back quickly; some don't.

'I'm fit and healthy,' he said. To prove it, he fastened his hands on the doorframe, pulled himself up, hung for a moment, grinned at her, and then dropped. 'I'm fine. Watch me.' He moved from the doorway one foot in front of the other, arms out at either side, eyes fixed on her. Midway across the room he toppled and then lurched, catching his hip on the table. Things flew. Milk dripped onto the floor.

He surveyed the damage with an expression of total neutrality and returned to his tightrope.

'Sit down, why don't you?' she said. 'Just a thought.'

He was concentrating on his feet.

Your leg. Fresh blood was welling up. She watched it bead, trace a route south.

'Did you notice my hair?' he asked. 'I didn't wash it once.' His hair was glossy, healthy. 'SPACE HAIR,' he said.

'Would a bath be a good thing?'

He spent the rest of the morning walking slowly around the house, patrolling the garden, sitting on the porch. She found it hard not to follow him around.

It was as if he had just got his sight back, the way he was looking at everything.

★

For a couple of weeks they were supposed to keep in touch with the base, stay local, though mornings were officially his own, and some afternoons might pan out that way too. The initial surge of activity was over.

At lunchtime he said, 'I'm going to meet the guys.' It was a statement. There was no suggestion that she should come along but she didn't stop to think about that.

'Just give me a second,' she said.

She found herself tucked in at a table with the team, dipping chicken wings and fries into ketchup and mayonnaise, alternating tumblers of Sprite with bottles of beer, listening as they recounted just what foods they missed the most up there. She was the only wife who had come along.

Corpse she knew well, and Shrink Fit, through reputation. Elvis and Gandalf and Steve Buscemi she had met only briefly, though she had absorbed the stories about them all. Originally a woman had been set for their mission, but she had to pull out.

'Oreos,' Elvis said.

'No,' said Gandalf. 'Someone always says Oreos. Can we get some more ketchup here?' He gesticulated to the waitress with the visual aid of

the empty bottle, put it back on the table in front
of him, and, looking circumspect, rotated it in the
palms of his hands. 'I hate the crust,' he said. 'Do
you see the crust on that?' He held the bottle up so
that everyone could get a proper look at the rim.

'Hey. Why don't you pass it round?' Steve
B said.

'Hey. Why don't they do something about
the crust?' said Gandalf.

'It's not the crust that bothers me,' Shrink Fit
said. 'It's that watery shit at the bottom.'

She glanced at him, sitting at the end of the
table, hands behind his head, legs outstretched.
He wasn't saying anything, but he looked happy
enough, just soaking it up. These are my guys, his
look seemed to be saying. It's all good.

'I get to choose,' Elvis said. 'It's my food.'

'It's everyone's food. You can't say Oreos,
man.' Shrink Fit reached for a fry, shaking his head
slowly, as if at some profound truth.

'Whose rules are these?' Elvis said. 'This is
bullshit.' He punctuated what seemed to be a
genuine frustration with a chicken wing that had
never quite made it to his mouth.

'Christ. Are we still on the fucking Oreos?'
Gandalf asked.

'You just can't say Oreos,' Shrink Fit said
again.

'Motherfucker,' said Elvis.

The waitress brought a new bottle of ketchup and set it in the middle of the table.

'Can I give you this? I hate looking at the crust.' Gandalf handed her the empty bottle, ignoring the look she gave him in return.

'The thing is,' he turned his attention to the table. 'And this is fundamental.' He set his hands palms down, as if laying down the law. 'You *get* the Oreos. Everyone gets the Oreos. It's a given. You get those for free. So you get to choose something else.' He gave Elvis a rictus smile. 'This is how you should think of it.'

'I don't see the problem with this,' Steve B said. 'Everyone's happy, right?'

'Everyone's happy.' Shrink Fit beat out a rhythm on the table top, grinning to himself.

She got up from the table, prompting a ripple of tut-tutting as she walked towards the door.

She was leaning forward, cupping her cigarette, trying to light it in the breeze, when she felt a pair of hands on her shoulders.

'El-ea-nor.' It was Corpse. 'Save me from these assholes.'

She smiled. He had always called her that, punishing her accent with a kind of mock-respect, as if she were royalty. The only other people who used her full name were her parents.

He put his hands on her shoulders and looked her up and down. He was a man who had never stopped looking like a teen; long-limbed and gangly. In the bright, clear sunlight he looked paler than ever – skin translucent, eyelashes near invisible. Even his freckles seemed to have faded.

'How's my girl?' he said, studying her face.

'Yeah,' she said, with a nod.

'Stick out your tongue, say "Ah",' he said.

'Ah,' she said.

'Fit as a fiddle. Right as rain,' he said.

He helped her light her cigarette and then lit one for himself, and they stood there together, looking out into the street, smoking and saying nothing. She watched the dust getting picked up in gusts at the side of the road and whirled in small circles around and around, like miniature cyclones. The sky was a cold blue, with vague wisps of cloud which seemed to her entirely static, seemed somehow to be grafted on up there.

She surprised herself by letting out a long, low sigh.

Corpse reached across and took her free hand in his. Their palms sat warm against each other. He leant back against the wall of the diner, and she did the same, and he closed his eyes, and she did the same, and together they felt the warmth of the sun on their skin.

'God that's good,' he said.

The alcohol went straight to all their heads. By late afternoon the astronauts were heading home for bed, tired out and fractious, like small boys.

He allowed her to help him up the stairs, and under the sheets, and then he was out.

★

He was awake in the night. She heard him banging around downstairs. Lying there in bed she tried to follow his movements in her mind. From the amount of noise she imagined a mess. When she woke up in the morning he was fast asleep beside her, and when she went down everything was clean, stowed.

She made toast, and walked in circles around the table in the kitchen, looking for some clue to what he'd done. Moving to the living room she traced her rotations around the edge of the carpet in the middle of the floor. It was bright, patterned, ugly; a wedding gift from one of his friends.

Late morning she tried to coax him out of sleep. She tickled his feet, his ribs. She sprinkled water on his face. She opened the window and let in fresh air. She pulled off the duvet and left it in a heap on the floor. She brought the light box from its place in the corner, held it to his face, and then gave up and just watched him breathe.

She wondered about calling one of the other wives. Instead, while he was sleeping, she tried to concentrate on her work.

When she had moved to the States she had continued working freelance, writing articles on anything that came her way. It had taken a while back home to build up a list that led to steady work – she'd been afraid to start over, but so far, touch wood, things had worked out.

She had to finish a piece on ecological housing. She sat on the bed with the laptop on her knees. As he slept on, she immersed herself in the odd beauty of homes made of earth and tyres, recycled bottles, aluminium cans. Come lunchtime she moved to the porch, and stayed until dusk, her notes spread along the weathered boards.

She woke the next day to find a row of refuse sacks in the hall. As she sat with his coffee on the edge of their bed he was smiling in his sleep.

'A spring clean?' she asked when he appeared. He looked confused. 'What's in the bags?' she said.

'Just stuff.'

'Like what?'

He shrugged, dismissive. 'I'm starving,' he said. 'What do we have?'

'I didn't hear anything,' she said.

He had the refrigerator door open, was looking in, pensive.

'Hey!' she said.

'Yeah.'

'I didn't hear a thing.'

His hand hovered over something in the fridge and then changed its mind. 'I was quiet as a mouse,' he said.

'You don't have to be. I don't mind. Make all the noise you like.'

'You were asleep.'

'I don't care. Wake me.'

The fridge started whining because the door had been open so long. 'What are you looking for?' she asked.

After breakfast he said he might as well head off to the refuse with those sacks.

'I'll drive you,' she said.

'No need.'

'I'd better drive you,' she said.

They loaded the trunk. At the refuse point she stayed in the car, watched the bags disappear one by one.

She phoned home. 'He finds it hard to talk about,' she told her mother.

'But it must be nice to have him back?'

'It is. It is. It is,' she said.

She was sitting in the hallway on an old wooden stool which creaked with every movement she made. She had her back against the wall to try to keep still but it just made things worse. She swung her feet down and walked towards the front door. It was open. She propped herself against the frame.

'Tell me,' her mother asked. 'Have you been interviewed by the media? You must have been approached?' She wanted her to put him on the line, so she could talk to him herself.

'He's at the base,' she told her mother, as she watched him pacing the garden looking like a man in love.

'Later, then,' her mother said. 'We'll be up.'

'There is something I have to tell you,' he had said, one day over coffee. This time they had met in Manhattan. They had been involved for two years. Two years of transatlantic crossings. New York was like meeting halfway, but it was clear now that something had to give.

He was nervous, which was unusual, and made her wonder what he was about to say. And then he had told her that he was very probably going to space, which was not what she had expected at all.

'So I'll move to the States,' she had said, resolutely. 'And then you'll move to space.'

They had spent the rest of the day at their hotel. She remembers the cool of the windowpane on her neck as they leant together up above the city.

'I don't know what to do,' she said.

'About what?'

'About you,' she said. He opened his eyes. He was flat out, lengthways, on the sofa. 'About your sleep.'

'It's fine,' he said.

'Is it normal?'

'Early days,' he said.

'Should we check?'

'Early days,' he said again. 'Forget about it.'

'Shouldn't you at least try to regulate? You're becoming nocturnal.' She was surprised at the tone of her voice.

He closed his eyes. 'Yeah. Don't feed me after midnight.'

'Your mother-in-law wants to talk,' she said, walking away.

★

She was awake anyway, but she heard the door, feet on the porch, the squeal of the first step. Switching on the bedside light she waited. She imagined his slow walk.

When he didn't show, she slipped on shoes and went out, walked the circumference of the house. She checked inside. Maybe she'd been mistaken, maybe he'd been coming in.

She walked to the end of the drive to check the car, and then stood on the verge, looking up and down the road.

She ran through the checklist in her head. She wondered whether she should call the base but knew he would be irritated. Only his sleep, she told herself, had really been affected. He hadn't been gone long. He couldn't have gone far.

She thought about taking the car, driving around the neighbourhood. She pictured herself behind the wheel, trawling the roads, calling his name. It seemed melodramatic.

Because she couldn't imagine going back

to sleep she waited, wrapped in the duvet on the porch. She forced herself to think about other things – her article, the man in Sedona she wanted to interview. She sketched a list of questions in her head.

She had always liked the idea of doing interviews but somehow had avoided them so far. She wondered whether she had the necessary pep to be convincing. She couldn't help comparing her relative reserve with the sunny side up, all-American smiles of the women she had come to know.

'Hello, I'm Eleanor Francis,' she said, with vim, extending her hand. 'How are you?' She tried to give the words an energetic spin so they volleyed off the tongue, suggesting untold resources in positive thinking and general can-do. She grinned at the imaginary figure whose fingers were clasped in her own. Her face began to hurt.

'You're up early,' he said. He was on the grass, looking up at her. The first rays of sunlight were edging across the lawn, licking at his bare feet.

'Right,' she said. She felt stoned with lack of sleep.

'I went for a walk.' He shifted his feet in and out of the light. 'I thought I should get some exercise.'

'Right,' she said.

'Gotta take a shower. My feet are really hot.'

He went inside.

★

She watched the sun rise in the corner of their room, stared hard at its white light.

'I'm going away for a few days,' she said, when he came out of the bathroom. 'I have to interview some guy for my work. OK?'

'A-OK.' He said, rolling into bed with his smile.

She enjoyed driving. She enjoyed waking each day in a new place, grabbing whatever breakfast they offered and then heading out on to the road.

The interstates were long and straight and pretty clear for good stretches. You could really put your foot down. Roads in England were never like this.

At first changes in the landscape were minor. She passed a sprawling procession of strip towns, with strip malls, and the usual run of roadside food stops: Wendy's, Taco Bell, McDonald's.

Later, when Route 40 took her back to New Mexico and through Albuquerque where they'd first lived, the land seemed to stretch and the sky seemed wide open.

'The shell, as you'll know,' he said, 'is tyres and earth packed together, plastered with adobe.'

He must have been in his sixties. He had shoulder-length white hair, tied back, and had about him a vitality that she found attractive. His skin was weathered – a lifetime spent outdoors.

They walked around the outside of the building together.

'The walls create the thermal mass,' he said. 'The heating and cooling system is completely independent. Inside it's warm in winter, cool in summer.'

They stopped and looked in at a long corridor of plants.

'The greenhouse hallway. South-facing. Waste water gets recycled in the planter.'

'You use pumice, right?'

'And the plants help oxygenate the water. We have vegetables, and some more exotic things.' She could see orchids, banana trees, palm fronds.

Inside was a miracle of sculpted walls and arches, intricate mosaics, rich foliage and water. If you hadn't seen it, you'd find it hard to believe: a sanctuary in this desert of sun-baked red earth.

She walked out a distance from the house with no purpose except to stand in the middle of that expanse; in that heat, on the dry earth. She looked back towards the building. It was like a pale, smooth pebble – like something you could hold in the palm of your hand.

On the terrace, in the evening, she sat with her back warm against the wall, her legs outstretched towards a rusty, shimmering horizon.

'The colour,' she said. 'What is that?'

'Red sandstone, iron oxide, quartz.'

They watched the light fade, the sky deepen. 'Out here,' he said, 'the night is a remarkable thing. You just watch.'

The temperature dropped. The darkness was infinite, spacious.

She woke early – awake the way she hadn't been since she was a child. She sat in bed, upright, listening to the pre-dawn quiet. She kept her eyes open to the dark, conscious of the warmth of the sheets under the soles of her feet, the cool air on her neck.

She wondered if her husband was awake too. She imagined him listening to the creaking of their timber-frame home. She tried to imagine what it was he saw as his eyes adjusted, the shapes that presented themselves.

The Dead Roads

D.W. Wilson

ONE TIME WE roadtripped across the country
with Animal Brooks, and he almost got run over
by a pickup truck partway through Alberta. It
was me and my twenty-year-old girlfriend Vic
and him, him in his cadpat jumpsuit, Vic in her
flannel logger coat and her neon hair that glowed
like a bush-lamp. We'd known Animal since
grade school: the north-born shitkicker, like Mick
Dundee. A lone ranger, or something. Then in
2002 the three of us crammed into his '67 Camaro
to tear-ass down the Trans-Canada at eighty miles
an hour. Vic and me had a couple hundred bucks
and time to kill before she went back to university.
That'd make it August, or just so. Animal had a
way of not caring too much and a way of hitting
on Vic. He was twenty-six and hunted looking,
with engine-grease stubble and red eyes sunk past
his cheekbones. In his commie hat and Converses
he had that hurting lurch, like a scrapper's swag,
dragging foot after foot with his knees loose and
his shoulders slumped. He'd drink a garden hose

under the table if it looked at him wrong. He once boned a girl in some poison ivy bushes, but was a gentleman about it. An ugly dent caved his forehead and rumours around Invermere said he'd been booted by a cow and then survived.

Vic stole shotgun right from the get-go and Animal preferred a girl beside him anyway, so I'd squished in the back among our gear. We had a ton of liquor but only a two-man tent because Animal didn't care one way. He'd packed nothing but his wallet and a bottle-rimmed copy of *The Once and Future King*, and he threatened to beat me to death with the Camaro's dipstick if he caught me touching his book. His brother used to read it to him before bed, and that made it an item of certain value, a real point of civic pride.

The Camaro's vinyl seats smelled like citrus cleaner. First time I ever got a girl pregnant was in Animal's backseat, but I didn't want to mention it since Vic would've ditched out then and there. Vic'll crack you with a highball glass if you say the wrong thing, she can do that. We weren't really dating, either. She just came home in the summers to visit her old man and score a few bucks slopping mortar, and we'd hook up. I don't know anyone prettier than Vic. She's got a heart-shaped face and sun freckles on her chin and a lazy eye when she drinks and these wineglass-sized breasts I get to look at sometimes. On the West Coast she bops around with a university kid who wears a sweater and carries a man purse. Her dad showed me a picture of the guy, all milk-jug ears and a pinched nose that'd bust easy in a fight. Upper-middle-class, horizon-in-his-irons, that type. Not that I can really complain, I guess. Vic never mentioned him and I never mentioned him and we went about our business like we used to, like when we were sixteen and bent together in the old fur-trading fort up the beach on Caribou Road.

Vic planned our journey with a 1980s road atlas she snagged from her dad's material shed. Animal kept his hand on the stick shift so he could zag around semis hauling B.C. Timber to the tar sands. Whenever he geared to fifth his palm plopped onto Vic's thigh. Each time, she'd swat him and give him the eyebrow and he'd wink at me in the rearview. —Dun worry, Duncan, I wouldn't do that to ya, he'd say, but I know Animal.

For the first day we plowed east through the national park. Cops don't patrol there so Animal went batshit. His Camaro handled like a motorbike and it packed enough horse to climb a hill in fifth, and I don't know if he let off the gun the whole way. He held a Kokanee between his legs and gulped it whenever the road straightened. Animal was a top-notch driver. As a job, he manned a cargo truck for this organic potato delivery service. One time he spun an e-brake slide at forty miles per hour, so me and him could chase down these highschoolers who'd hucked a butternut squash through his windshield.

To kill time, Animal bought a *Playboy* and handed it to Vic. He suggested she do a dramatic read if possible. At first she gave him the eye, but he threatened to have me do it if not her. He also handed her all the receipts for gas and food and booze to keep track of, on account of her higher education, but I'm not even sure Vic did much math. At university she studied biology and swamplands, and I like to think I got her into it, since there's a great wide marsh behind this place we used to get shitfaced at. It's a panelboard bungalow on the outskirts of town, built, Vic figures, on floodland from the Sevenhead River. Vic and me used to stash our weed in the water, pinned under the vegetation band. One time we stole election signs and ditched them in the marsh, and the *Valley Echo* printed a headline that said the cops didn't know to call it vandalism or a political statement. Neither did I really, since Vic planned the whole thing. Then last summer I asked her to muck around the marsh with me but she said we really shouldn't, because it's drying up. She had a bunch of science to prove it. —Something has to change, Dunc, she said, pawing at me. —Or there'll be nothing left.

Eventually Animal bored of the Trans-Canada, so he veered onto some single-lane switchback that traced the Rocky Mountains north. I thought Vic'd be distressed but turned out she expected it. She shoved the road atlas under the seat and dug a baggie of weed from her pack. Later, we played punch buggy, but I couldn't see much from the back and Vic walloped me on the charley horse so goddamn hard I got gooseskins straight down to my toes.

★

The sign said, *Tent Camping – $15*, and Animal said, —Fuck that shit, and then he booted the sign pole, for good measure. He plunked himself on the Camaro's cobalt hood and rubbed his eyes. We'd been on the road for a while, and I don't remember if he ever slept much. The air smelled like forest fire and it also reeked of cow shit, but Alberta usually reeks of cow shit. Vic leaned into the door frame, hip cocked to one side like a teenager. Her flannel sleeves hung too low and she bunched the extra fabric in each fist. She chewed a piece of her hair. When we used to date I would tug those strands out of her mouth and she'd ruck her eyebrows to a scowl and I'd scramble away before she belted me one. It was starting to turn to evening. In the low Albertan dusk her bright hair shone the colour of whiskey. She caught me staring, winked.

Vic slid her hands in her jean pockets. —I got fifteen bucks.

—Yeah I bet ya do, Animal said.

—What the hell does that mean?

—Et's Duncan's cash, enn'it?

—Just some, Vic said.

—I got more money 'en Duncan, ya know.

—Shut your mouth, Animal, I told him.

—Jus sayin, he said, and ducked into the driver seat.

We reached someplace called Shellyoak and Animal called all eyes on the lookout for a campsite. He drove through the town's main haul, where the Camaro's wide nose spanned the lane past centre. A ways out, the Rockies marked the border home. This far north their surfaces were dotted with pine husks – grey, chewed-out shells left over from the pine beetle plague. Not a living tree in sight. Shellyoak's buildings were slate brick with round chimneys and tiny windows high as a man's chin. A group of kids smoked dope on a street bench and Vic hollered for directions and one waved up the lane with an arm so skinny it flailed like an elastic.

—Near the amusement park, he called.

Big rocks broke the landscape on Shellyoak's outskirts, and Vic figured it used to be under a glacier. Animal was dead silent the whole way. I guess the bony trees irked him, that carcass forest. The stink of woodsmoke blasted from the fan and it reminded me of the chimneys that burned when I used to scrape frost off Vic's windshield, all those mornings after I stayed the night at her place. One time her dad was in the kitchen as I tried to sneak out, and he handed me a coffee and some ice shears and told me to keep in his good books. Then he said Vic and me made a good pair, us two, but if I got her pregnant he'd probably beat me to death with an extension cord. He grinned like a boy, I remember. Then he said, —Seriously though, ya make a good pair. A few minutes later Vic tiptoed downstairs and her old man clapped me on the shoulder like a son, and Vic smiled as if she could be happier than ever.

Animal yawed us around a bend and all at once the horizon lit up with a neon clown head big as an RV. From our angle, it looked as if the clown also had rabbit ears, flopped down like two bendy fluorescent scoops. The highway'd gone gravel and the Camaro's tires pinged pebbles on the undercarriage. In the distance I saw a Ferris wheel rocking like a treetop, but not much else in the park to speak of. Animal geared down and this time when he laid his palm on Vic's knee he didn't take it off, and she didn't smack him. He still winked at me in the rearview, though. A second later Vic shook his hand away.

—Christ, it's a gas station too, Vic said, pointing at the pumps hidden in the clown's shadow. Animal steered toward them, tapped the fuel gauge with its needle at quarter-tank.

—You've got enough, I said, but he didn't so much as grunt.

He parked at the first pump and unfolded from the vehicle. Vic popped her seat forward so I could climb out. Figures milled inside the gas station and their outlines peered through the glass. A painted sign that said *Tickets, 5 bucks* hung above the door. On it, somebody'd drawn a moose.

Animal started pumping gas. He tweaked his eyebrows at me. —Well?

—The hell do you want now, I said.

—Go enside and ask where we ken camp, he said, then he winked over my shoulder, at Vic. —Giddyup now.

—They'll tell us to go to the pay grounds.

—Kid said we ken camp near the amusement park.

—That kid was on dope, I said.

—Yer on dope, he shot, and *thrump*ed his fingers on the Camaro's hood. He flashed his gums. —Go on, Skinny.

—What the fuck, Animal.

—Yer in muh way, Skinny, he said, and cocked his head to indicate Vic. —I seen better windows 'en you.

Then the station's stormdoor clattered and Vic yelped and I turned and saw the biggest goddamn Native man ever. He wore Carhartts and steeltoes and no shirt beneath the straps. The buckles dimpled his collar. His hair gummied to his cheeks and his head tilted at an angle. This gruesome, spider-like scar spanned his chest and the whole left nipple was sliced off, snubbed like a button nose. He leaned an arm-length calliper on his neck. Then his face jerked into a smile, but not a friendly kind. —I never seen a Camaro can run on diesel, he said, stressing his e's.

For a second he stood there in the doorway as if he might say *gotcha!* Vic bunched excess sleeve in her fists and I sniffed the air to see if the place reeked like diesel engines. And there it was: the smell of carbide and tar and dirty steel. Animal stared straight at the Native guy, as if in a game of chicken instead of wrecking his engine with the wrong fuel, as if he just needed to overcome something besides the way things actually were, as if he could just *be* stubborn enough. Then he killed the pump and yanked the nozzle from his tank.

—Where the fuck's et say?

The guy did a shrug-a-lug. —It's a trucker stop.

—Yeah well I'm notta trucker.

—Me neither, the guy said, and moved between Vic and me, toward the car, and the air that wafted after him stunk of B.O.. His neck muscles strained to hold his head straight, like he was used to keeping it down. A scrapper's stance, almost. I caught Vic's attention and her forehead scrunched up and the skin at her eyes tightened like old leather. I'd never known her to be the worrying type.

—Nice car though, the guy said. He dragged a wide hand over the Camaro's cobalt finish.

—Yeah et is.

—I'm Walla, he said, and swung his head to Vic. —This your girlfriend?

Animal banged his commie hat against his knuckles. —Ya got a pump er sompthen?

—Nup, Walla said, and stressed the p.

—Or sompthen else?

—Buddy has a siphon.

—Ken we get et?

—Nup, getting too late, he said, and pointed with one sausage finger at the darkening sky.

—Tomorrow, I bet.

Animal's mouth jawed in circles and I could all but hear his brain trying to find a way to make it all go right. —There a campsite nearby? I said, to buy time.

Walla twitched his head behind him. —The summit. Not like she's a real mountain, though. You owe me twelve thirty-seven for the diesel.

—The hells I do, Animal said, and crossed his arms.

Walla set the callipers on the Camaro's hood and their measurement end *tink*ed. He swung his gaze from me to Animal to Vic, then to Animal and then at the shop. He stood nearest Vic of all, a full two and a half heads taller than her, and I swear to God he had hands big as mudflaps. —No, he said, very slowly, —you do.

Vic dug cash from her wallet, fifteen bucks. She handed it over and Walla tugged the bills from her one at a time. —I'll get your change, he said, and stepped toward the station. Then, over his shoulder: —You can't leave your car there. He grinned at Vic and his teeth were white as gold. —Well, maybe you can. Push her outta the way of the pump.

I got behind the Camaro. Animal hung at the gas tank like one of those old guys who hope somebody'll come talk to them. —Put her in neutral, idiot, I snapped, and dug my toes into the ground and heaved and the Camaro rocked. Vic pressed her back to the bumper. —What's happening? she whispered to me, but I grunted and got the car rolling and hoped I didn't have to scrap with Walla.

We pushed the Camaro outside the clown face's shadow and I put myself between Vic and the station. Walla reappeared, horselike in his gait. He dumped the coins in my palm and ran his tongue over his teeth. He touched a notch under his jaw. —The summit'd be a helluva climb, he said. —Especially if you're taking your booze. I got a pickup.

—We can hike it, I said.

—Trade you a lift.

—Fer what, Animal barked.

—What ya got? Walla said, and rubbed his triceps. The scar tissue on his chest looked sun-dried, pinker than it ought to, and in the sticky neon light it shone raw and oily like a beating. —Aw hell, he said, —I'll help you out. Get yer stuff.

We grabbed our beer cooler and Vic took the sleeping bag and Animal pocketed *The Once and Future King*. Walla disappeared around the gas station and a few minutes later he came chewing up gravel in a green three-seater Dodge. He was sardined in driver with his shoulders hunched and his knees against his armpits. The truck had a bust-out rear window and poly duct-taped in the gap. Horse quilts blanketed the box, warm with the smell of dog.

　　—One of you needs to sit in the bed, Walla said, then dangled his keys, —and one of you needs to drive, cause I'm shittered and the fucking pigs have it out for me.

　　Animal lunged for the keys and me and him shared this moment between us, his mouth twisted like a grin, and I wanted to hit him so bad. But if I whaled on him I'd look bad to Vic, so I climbed into the mess of bedding while Animal drove the switchback. The truck whipped around bends and I imagined Walla's skunky B.O. sneaking through the patched-up window, how bad it must've been in the cab with him. Animal was goddamn lucky he'd pocketed his book. The whole way, Vic shifted uncomfortably, and I could hear her thighs brushing Walla on one side and Animal on the other.

★

We got to the summit when the sun tucked under the Rockies and everything went grey and dead-looking as the forest. Walla showed us a firepit ringed by skeleton trees where he'd piled some chopped wood. Animal collapsed near the pit to work a blaze. He waved Vic off when she offered to help, so she dug a mickey of Canadian Club from the cooler. Fifty feet off, a cliff dropped to the highway below, where the Ferris wheel keeled and the goddamn clown face smirked.

—Thanks for helping us, Vic said. She sat down on an upturned log, whiskey on her knee.

—My dad tells me if you're cooking stew, and you don't put meat in it, you can't bitch when yer eating it, Walla said, and he grinned to show his pearly teeth, and Vic laughed and so did I, though I didn't know what the hell he meant. Then he said:

—Now I need a lift down to the station.

Vic froze in the middle of sipping her whiskey and Animal looked up from his smouldering fire.

—What'dya mean.

—I told you, I'm shittered, and the pigs have it out for me.

—I'm buildin the fire, Animal said, but Walla had his eyes on Vic, anyway. Vic glanced from Walla to me and I knew she wouldn't ask me to step in, because she won't do that, ever. One time she figured out how to fix a circuit fault on her Ranger all her own, because she didn't want to ask her old man how.

—I'll do it, I said to Walla, and then I dumped my half-empty beer over Animal's wimpy fire and he threatened to beat me to death with the kindling.

Walla flicked me his keys and I palmed them from the air and got in the driver seat, and he swung into passenger like a buddy. Not thirty seconds into the drive his stench soured up the cab, but at least he smelled like a working man, like he just forgot to shower, and not like some hobo. On the way down, the poly over the rear panel smacked about and more than once he leaned sideways to inspect the tape. He spread one leg across the seat, draped his arm clear out the window, and I wondered if his knuckles bobbed along the gravel. In the distance, the horizon glowed from the park lights and the treetops resembled hundreds of heated needles. I kept the highbeams on and scanned for marble eyes, since twilight is the worst time for hitting deer, but Walla told me that all the deer fled north with the beetles. —Nothin here but us and the flies, he said. —A thousand dead acres.

—The dead roads, or something.

—I don't mind that, Walla said. Then: —They're an odd couple, eh?

—Who.

—The girl and him, Animal.

—They're not a couple.

—The way he looks at her? Sure they are. Or gonna be, he said, and punched me on the arm like we were friends.

—He looks at all girls like that.

Walla smiled like a Mason jar. He had fillings in his teeth. —Her, too. She was lookin at him too.

The station and the clown face swept into view, and as I geared down my fist touched Walla's knee. Vic had about zero reason to go for a guy like Animal, so I don't know. But then I imagined the two of them bent together at that shitty fire, red marks scraped over Vic's neck and collarbones from Animal's barbed-wire stubble.

—You got a thing for her, eh, Walla said.

—No.

—Might be you need to take him down a notch.

—We're buds, I said, and parked the truck.

Walla extracted himself from the passenger seat. —Nah man, he said from across the hood. —*We're* buds.

Whatever the hell he meant I'll never know, since I ditched him and started back along the road, toward the summit. The whole way I thought about Animal and Vic and I tried not think about them at the same time. I'd known them so long - my two best friends, really. The outside smelled more like driftwood than a forest. Wind kicked dirt at my face and though it breezed around the treetops they just creaked like power poles. I wouldn't have been surprised if a goddamn wolfman came pounding out of the dark. A few times headlights tear-assed up the road and a few times I almost barrelled sideways and I just got madder even thinking of it.

Then the slope evened out, which meant I neared the summit, and then the trees flickered campfire-orange. The road looped our campsite so I cut through the forest. Never been so scared in my life, those last steps. Animal atop Vic, grinding away, probably still in his stupid commie hat and his Converses - no sight in the world could be worse.

I'd rather get shot. Walla was right – Animal'd been gunning for her the whole trip. Right from the start when he kicked me to the backseat, some big plan – some big, selfish plan.

I got close enough to see the flames. Vic sat under her sleeping bag, off near the cliff edge, but I could only make out her outline in the orange light. Animal was MIA. They might have already finished, how could I know. I crept along the tree line, scanned for him. Not sure what I hoped to accomplish. It's not like he kept a dark secret.

I found him outside the campsite with his back to the slope and his cock in his hand and a stream of piss splattering on a tree. It was dark enough that I didn't get the whole picture, thank God for that. He'd crossed the road to make use of a big pine that might have been a little bit alive – for some reason Animal really didn't like those dead trees. I had some things to say to him. Vic's old man once told me a guy needs to know when to pick his battles, and as I watched Animal, pissing as if nothing mattered, I figured it out: a guy needs to know what he cares about most, and Animal, well, he didn't care about stuff. But he had to know I did. Christ, everybody in the valley knew I did. It'd be like if I tried to steal his car for a joyride. I'm his friend, for fucker's sake.

Then a truck hauled ass up the road, kicking gravel in a spray. It had a good clip and its rear end fishtailed, out of control or so the passengers could get a laugh. Its headlamps swung around, but on

that switchback the dead trees scattered the light
– no way the driver would see Animal, not before
clobbering him. Animal turned as if to check what
the commotion was about. Either he couldn't see
or he was too stupid to dive for cover or he figured
no truck would dare to run him down. I saw the
trajectory, though, loud and clear: the pickup's
rear end would swing into him, knock him ass-
over-teakettle into the woods, and that'd be that
for Animal Brooks. But I didn't yell out. I didn't
make a sound. Because all I could think of was his
hand on Vic's thigh, over and over the whole trip,
his wild grin in the rearview and all the stuff he'd
pulled to be alone with her. So nope, I didn't yell
out, and the truck fishtailed right toward him and
he yowled like a dog and I lost track of where he
went.

Vic bolted from the tree line, almost right
into me, and I scrambled after her. She gave me a
look, as if surprised, but I just nodded like I ought
to be there. Animal had already clambered to his
feet. Moss and dead twigs stuck to his face, and his
commie hat had been biffed away and the forest
floor was beat up where he'd rolled across it. He
pulled a pinecone from his hair and stared at it in
wonder.

—Animal, Vic barked. —You okay?

He flicked the pinecone aside, seemed to
notice us. —Why the hell didn't ya say sompthen,
he said, staring at me.

—What?

—Yuh were across the road. Why didn't ya yell out or sompthen. Fucken truck nearly killed me.

—I just got here, I told him.

—Ya just got here, eh.

—Yeah, got back right now.

Animal swiped his commie hat from the ground. He banged it against his thigh to dust it off. —Just en time to see my kung fu reflexes, he said, and grinned.

—So you're okay? Vic said.

—Shaken up, yeah.

Vic grabbed Animal's chin and turned his head sideways. His cheek was scraped and dirty and Vic licked her thumb to rub it clean. —Mighta pulled a groin muscle, too, he said when she stepped back, and Vic lasted a full two seconds of his leer before she punched him in the chest hard enough to make him wheeze.

★

Afterward, by the fire, Animal shook out his adrenalin. —Woulda sucked to run that truck over, he said, and laughed, a deep, throaty laugh like a guy does when he's survived an event that should have killed him. Then he dug into the cooler and started skulling beers to drown his jitters.

Vic and me shared the mickey of Canadian Club, away from the campfire so we could look over the cliffside at this bizarre piece of land. She took a big chug from the bottle and handed it over. Vic can drink like a tradesman when times come. The moonlight made her cheeks silver and that lazy eye of hers acted out. She spread her sleeping bag across her legs and I inched my way under it and the nylon clung to my shins. Vic smelled like a campfire. Vic smelled like citrus shampoo or something. Vic smelled like Vic.

—This an alright place to sleep, she said and wiggled in the dirt and the dried bloodweed and made a little nest.

—I'm not picky, I said.

—You smell like a dog.

—Sorry, Vic.

She belted me on the shoulder and I leaned into her. Below us a couple semis zoomed north and the Ferris wheel spun and I thought I could hear Walla chopping lumber. Christ, a weirder place. By the fire, Animal sounded out words from his book, finger under each sentence. Then Vic unbuttoned her flannel coat. She always wore it or if not the coat then a flannel shirt. Sexiest thing, swear to God. I remember how she took it off, first time we ever boned, all awkward and struggling so I had to help her with the sleeves. A different kind of time back then. A different way of going about things, even. Sometimes I wish I was smarter so I could've gone to university with Vic.

Vic put her hand under my chin and jacked my head to eye level. I guess I was looking at her breasts. She leaned in and kissed me and she tasted like dope, and softness, and her smooth chin ground on my middle-of-the-night stubble. But I couldn't kiss her right then. I don't know why. She slicked her tongue over my lips and I couldn't get my head around the whole thing, the Ferris wheel and what Walla said and how I almost got Animal killed, and Vic, you know, and the whole goddamn thing.

—Don't fuck around, she said, but the words were all breath.

—Just thinkin is all.

She bit down on my lip. —Well, stop it.

—I like you a lot, Vic.

For a second she stopped and turned her head and her neon hair grazed my nose and I'd have given anything to know what was going on in her head right then. She had her lips squished shut and her forehead a little scrunched as if figuring something out - same look as the day she left for university. That'd have been in '99, and her and her old man and me stayed at a hotel in Calgary so she could catch her West Coast flight in the wee hours, and while she showered, her old man told me not to let her get away. —It'll happen, Duncan, he said, his face drawn in and lined around his eyes, as if he knew what the hell he was talking about. —I swear to God you'll lose her if you don't take action soon. And I nodded and tried not to grin, because I understood exactly what he meant.

On the mountaintop, Vic hooked hair behind her ear. —You're my guy, Dunc, she said as though it were true.

 —I know, Vic. But sometimes I don't know. You know?

 Then she cuffed me, all playful, and pulled me into her.

 But that's Vic for you. Afterward, when we were done and Animal's moans were snores and the fire glowed down to embers, Vic sat up and stretched. Her ribs made bumps under her skin and the muscles along her spine tensed and eased and it felt alright right then. That's Vic for you, that's how she can make you feel, that easy. Never liked a girl so much. Nothing else to it. I just cared about her more than the university guy did or Animal did or maybe her old man did. I should've told her so, or how I wished she didn't have to go west, or how I'd had a ring for her for years but lacked the balls to do anything with it. Even then, the mountaintop seemed like a last chance or something.

 She sucked the rest of the whiskey and pointed at the sky where a trail of turquoise streaked across the horizon – the northern lights, earlier than I'd ever known them. She just stood there for a second with her back to me and those lights around her. Christ, she was so pretty. Then she whipped the empty bottle off the summit, and I stared at her and thought about her and waited for the sound of the bottle breaking way, way below us.

The Authors

M.J. Hyland's first novel, *How the Light Gets In* (2003), was shortlisted for the Commonwealth Writers' Prize. Her second, *Carry Me Down* (2006), won the Hawthornden and Encore Prizes and was shortlisted for the Man Booker Prize. Her third novel, *This is How* (2009), was longlisted for the Orange Prize and the International IMPAC Prize. Her short fiction has been published in *Zoetrope: All Story*, *BlackBook Magazine* (USA), *Best Australian Short Stories* and elsewhere. Her non-fiction regularly features in publications such as *London Review of Books*, *Irish Independent* and the *Financial Times*.

She worked for seven years as a commercial lawyer, and a lecturer in criminal law, before her first novel was published. She has also worked as an assistant director in film and television, and as a cadet journalist. She is currently a lecturer in creative writing in the Centre for New Writing, at the University of Manchester.

Alison MacLeod's short fiction has been published in a wide range of magazines including *Prospect*, *London Magazine*, *The Sunday Times* online magazine, in anthologies such as *The New Uncanny* and *Litmus* (both Comma) and broadcast on the BBC. A story from her most recent book, *Fifteen Modern Tales of Attraction*, 'Dirty Weekend', was awarded the Society of Authors'

Olive Cook Prize for Short Fiction. She is also the author of two novels, *The Changeling* (1996) and *The Wave Theory of Angels* (2005), and has won Writers' Awards from both Arts Council England and the Canada Council for the Arts.

His next novel will be published by Penguin in September 2012 and is set in Brighton, where she now lives and lectures on a part-time basis at the University of Chichester. She is currently completing her second short story collection.

Jon McGregor was born in 1976 and graduated from the University of Bradford with a BSc in Media Technology. Since 1999 he has built a career as a novelist and short story writer, publishing *If Nobody Speaks of Remarkable Things* (2002), *So Many Ways To Begin* (2006), and *Even The Dogs* (2010), which between them have won the Somerset Maugham Award and been twice long listed for the Man Booker Prize. He has also written for the *Guardian*, *The Observer*, *The Times*, *The New York Times* and *Granta* magazine.

His story collection *This Isn't The Sort of Thing That Happens to Someone Like You,* will be published in February 2012. He was a co-founder of the Nottingham Writers' Studio, and has been a writer-in-residence with the British Antarctic Survey, the Santa Maddalena Foundation, and, through the First Story organisation, Ellis Guilford School in Nottingham. In July 2011 he was made an honorary Doctor of Letters at the University of Nottingham.

K.J. Orr was born in London. As an undergraduate, she won the Dan Hemingway Prize at the University of St Andrews for a short story later published in the collection *Doris Lumsden's Heart-Shaped Bed & Other Stories* (2004). Her work has also appeared in the anthology *Cheque Enclosed* (2007) and the Bridport Prize collection 2010. She has won awards for both short fiction and plays, and been shortlisted for the London Writers' Prize, the Asham Award and the Bridport Prize.

She is a graduate of the MA in Creative Writing at the University of East Anglia and in 2010 won Arts and Humanities Research Council funding for a collection of short stories, as part of a PhD on the form at the University of Chichester. She divides her time between London and Chichester.

D.W. Wilson's first book, a collection of short stories titled *Once You Break a Knuckle*, is published this autumn by Penguin Canada, to be followed next year by a novel, *Ballistics*. His fiction and essays have appeared in literary journals across Canada, Ireland, and the United Kingdom. In 2008, he won the silver award for fiction at the Canadian National Magazine Awards, and this year he has been shortlisted for the Writers' Trust of Canada Journey Prize – the most prestigious award for emerging authors in Canada.

He studied creative writing at the University of East Anglia, where he was the recipient of the MA programme's inaugural Man Booker Prize Scholarship.